The Real People

A Young Woman's True Adventure Story to the Bering Sea

A.D. Winslow

The Real People
Copyright © 2022 by A.D. Winslow

ISBN
978-1-958122-42-6 (Paperback)
978-1-958122-41-9 (eBook)

Table of Contents

Chapter

Eight in the morning on my late day shift of work. I'm a ranger naturalist in Glacier National Park, Montana.

"Emmy," I hear my name softly through my bedroom door. My dad is visiting from Connecticut. My eyes open from the warm summer sun lighting up the old room with high ceilings and hard wood floors. It's sparsely decorated by some raggedy posters that I carry with me on my moves from Connecticut to Michigan and to Montana. I snuggle farther under my down comforter on this relatively warm mountain morning.

"You have a visitor," my dad says with a controlled calmness.

"Who is it?" I ask wondering who on this ranger compound would come over early. Everyone knows I love sleeping in on my late day shifts.

"It's Scott."

"Scott?" I ask.

"Scott." My dad says.

I look around the room at my antique rocking chair, at y knitting supplies, at my green back pack and at my muddy hiking boots. Scott?

I sit up on the mattress on the floor placing my feet together on the small antique oriental rug. Scott? The question becomes more perplexing as I stand up and walk to the bathroom. My heart beat becomes obvious to me as I wonder…Scott Powell?

He had pursued me three summers ago when I was a tour boat captain and he was a backcountry ranger. I finally took him up on a dinner offer half way through the summer. Although I remember feeling badly about going because I told another friend that I would eat in the cafeteria that night. Scott convinced me I was sad or crazy to eat in a cafeteria instead of having a home cooked meal. Maybe I thought he'd stop asking me if I went once to his ranger apartment.

I dress still half asleep and descend the broad staircase weaving from one side to the other. After turning the corner to the dining room I see Scott Powell leaning nervously against the window while my dad respectively tries to disappear into his cereal bowl.

Scott's deep set, dark blue eyes stare at my rosy cheek face. His clasped hands tentatively release each other for a hug. I put out my hand to shake his hand and offer him breakfast. I haven't seen him since his first surprise visit from Alaska last winter when I was teaching winter ecology here on the west side of Glacier.

After fumbling to get the new package of bacon open and fry it up I take the breakfast out to the picnic table overlooking the river. All spring the muddy river raged from the run off. We had had a lot of snow this winter but now in July the river has a clear, gentler flow giving way to the view of the red, yellow and blue sedimentary rocks that have crumbled from the mountain tops over millions of years. I thought Scott would show up when the river cleared.

I look up to the mountains. They had to go through about a billion years of violent activity to become the awesome landscape that it is today. Scott looks up to them curiously and then back to me.

Filling all the clear space on my flowered plate with syrup I look across the picnic table to Scott neatly wrapping his bacon in the pancake with a drop of syrup.

"I like sandwiches," he says taking an enthusiastic bite. My mom stops in the car by our picnic table in the grass and rolls down the window.

"Do you want some coffee, Scott? I'm going to get some."

"No thank you." He says with his cute Philidelphia accent.

"You're not a coffee drinker either?"

Scott and I look at each other for a moment with a shared fatique/ nervousness.

"What are you going to do this fall?" he asks.

"I'm looking for a teaching job but there isn't anything available here and they won't interview over the phone in Connecticut so I don't know."

"You should teach in Alaska. They need teachers there."

Cautiously I nod to his suggestion having thought about it myself. And wishing I hadn't been just his summer twinkie. His real woman was in Alaska the summer he wooed me. She was kept a secret to me til the end of the summer. Good grief.

Scott and I discuss the prospect of teaching in Alaska more at the bar tonight but he leaves the next day for British Columbia before learning the outcome or my growing interest. The mountains and exploration always attract me. Even in the Connecticut suburban town I grew up in I found ways to explore via sewer routes beneath the main streets of town. And ever since first grade I've wanted to be a teacher. After my four months of student teaching first grade with Mrs. Moore, she told me, "You have the love. *That* you can't teach."

I call the Alaska board of Education and they say they still need teachers in the Bush where ever that is but I am excited they have openings. The woman in Anchorage gives me a number to call in Bethel, Alaska. Gleefully I flip the pages picturing mountains, bears and volcanoes in a book of Alaska.

Two days later I call the Lower Kuskokwim School District. I hold the phone tightly to my ear trying to hear everything the secretary is saying through our delayed connection. Even though her speech is slow and soft the phone connection cuts us off so I call again.

"I'm looking for a teaching job."

"Yes…" she says kindly.

"Yes…" I say wishing she'd initiate some more information as I stand in the middle of my bedroom staring at the light fixture in my park service uniform. It's probably the best outfit I own for size and durability. All my other pants are baggy but these flatter my somewhat long, lean legs. The best thing about this uniform is I just throw it on in the morning. If I get a teaching job what will I wear? I stop my rambling thoughts as I wait for more information but there is none.

"I was told you need teachers. Is that true?"

"Let me take your number and I'll have someone call you back," she says slowly.

"Well, is there a better time to call later?" I ask fearing no one will call me back. Plus, we are two hours apart and I'm usually outside.

"Terence is in a meeting now but he should be back in a half hour," she says slowly.

"Okay thank you I'll try back then." I put down the old phone I borrowed from another seasonal ranger and squeeze my hands together.

Another couple of anxious days pass before I get in touch with Terence Harris who I assume is in charge of human resources.

"Hello," he says in a voice sounding like a lower 48 easterner like myself.

"Hello, my name is Emily Strauss and I'm interested in an elementary teaching position, I was told you have some positions available."

"Yes, we have three spots open. Do you have your Alaska teaching certificate?" he asks in a slightly slow and deep voice.

"No but I think my Michigan certificate has reciprocity with Alaska."

"No, you'd need to get an Alaska certificate but we could put that on the first priority list and hire you as a substitute. School starts tomorrow. Do you know how soon you could get here?" he asks. That's all he wants to know? How soon I can get there?

"Whenever I can get a flight."

"All right, we've got a position for fourth grade in Eek and Aniak and fifth grade position in Edinak with ten students. When would be a good time for you to interview?"

"Tomorrow until noon would be fine," I say thinking school starts tomorrow and you need more teachers. Just hire me now!

"Okay, I'll call you then. Just fax me your resume." After I hang up the phone, I pull out my education files and hints and rules for interviewing. I read everything over and have another ranger practice with me who is a retired teacher. I write down some questions for Terence as well as look up the places he told me they need teachers. Two are in land from the Bering Sea but Edinak is right next to the Bering Sea at about 60 degrees north latitude. That's where I want to go.

I sit by the phone until 10:30AM with a neat French braid in my wavy dark hair. I pressed my uniform twice this morning and am ready for work. 11:00 AM and I fear he won't call so I dial the number with all my notes before me.

"Hello, Terence Harris please?" A pause and then softly a response.

"Hold on please." I am disconnected. I try again and again and am connected on the third call.

"Oh, hello Emily, I was just getting ready to call you. Can I call you back in a few minutes?" he asks.

"We can just have the interview now if that's okay with you?" I offer. He clears his throat and possibly a chuckle.

"Okay, let me get my notes and find your resume."

After a few typical questions about my education history and philosophy he changes the line of questions.

"Have you ever been a minority?"

"Yes. In Ann Arbor I went with one of my friends to a Latin dance celebration and took an Islam course where I was the only Christian. I also cater Jewish holidays for one of my childhood friends and go to Blackfeet elk roasts here in Montana."

"Do you have any prejudices?" Terence asks.

"No, I take each person as their own person and get to know them given the opportunity."

"Do you know anything about the Eskimos and the Bush?"

"Just a little bit, but I could try to research before I get there."

"Have you ever lived without plumbing?" he continues in what I'm starting to think is a weird line of questions for a teaching job.

"Yes. For two summers as a boat captain, we had sporadic plumbing and electricity. It didn't bother me at all."

"Let me connect you to the principal. He's a real gentleman from Texas. His name is T.J. Sheehan."

The line breaks a little then I hear a friendly, deep and husky southern accent.

"Hello, this is T.J. Sheehan here."

"Hello, this is Emily Strauss…how are you?"

"Well, I'll tell you. I'm up to my elbows in alligators. How are you?" he asks in a fatherly, jovial tone.

"I'm fine," I say tickled by his expression wondering what faces match these voices.

"Well, Emily," he says in a gentle voice," I have just one question for you…are you tough?" he asks emphasizing tough in a good humored tone. I smile to myself contemplating the question with one memory.

It was the week before I was to return to college three summers ago. I was trying to write a letter to Scott next to a stream in Logan Pass' alpine meadow. Purple asters, crimson Indian paintbrushes and yellow cinquefoil were my only company.

The Sun was shining late in the afternoon as well as the crescent Moon. A light breeze cooled my face while my feet cooled off in the stream. My boots and back pack supported my back as I hunched over my journal and this letter to Scott. I looked at the paper then up to the mountain peaks around me all unique in their forms. One like a horn behind me carved away by glaciers on three sides and one to the left of me shaped like the profile of a gorilla's head. Before me lay the continental divide. The wall in the Rocky Mountains separating the watersheds in to the Pacific and Atlantic. To my right spread the St. Mary Valley. Mountains like curtains fell in along the stretch of water opening out to the plains on the east side of the park.

Breathing in the clean air, looking back at the stalled letter…I shied up again. How do I tell Scott the happiness he ended up bringing me before I go back to school? I looked up again to my left.

There. Five feet away was a grizzly bear. Watching me.

My heart dropped.

"Hey bear," I said softly. I know you were supposed to talk quietly and not run. The bear continued to walk towards me slowly looking right into my eyes. Slowly I rolled onto my side into a loose fetal position while feeling like my skin was turning inside out. I glared at my pounding heart to shut up and waited. After a moment of nothing I thought maybe the bear had gone. I peered towards the stream. Only the wild flowers swayed on the other side. Then a splash from behind me. I turned my head and peeked under my arm. Now ten feet back was the grizzly laying down in a small pool with my back pack under his chin and his snout in my boot. My favorite black sweater stretched a little less than the distance between the grizzly and me.

Then the grizzly withdrew his snout from my boot. He looked over at me spying on him. Quickly I looked down. Eye contact was a challenging and threatening gesture. Then I looked back again. Now his long, finger-like yellow claws and big, sharp, white teeth meticulously pulled at the hinge on the film door of my camera. His huge, strong shoulder muscles rippled underneath his milk chocolate colored fur as he grappled with the camera. Again, he looked at me. I looked down wondering how to escape smelling the coldness of the rock that had become my island. I checked the bear one more time thinking I could inch away if his attention stayed with the contents of my green back pack. This time when the bear saw my eyes he stood up and started walking towards me slowly holding my gaze.

His broad face matched the size of his head, well placed ears and beautiful eyes. Alternating shades of brown stripes in his irises. We kept looking at each other until he was above me and all I could see were massive paws and the last step placing the tip of his four inch claws under my shoulder. Turning my head to the rock I thought, "Okay…I've had a good life." His warm, thick breath moved from my neck slowly down to my hips and then back up. "Wait, please don't eat me." I prayed. Slowly I pulled up my right shoulder blade to stick my ribs out and be less edible. A gentle nudge from the grizzly's snout pushed up against that shoulder blade. I waited for teeth but felt nothing. Instead, I looked up to the sound of the rustling vegetation in front of me. Walking away was the little tail on that great grizzly bear.

"Yes, I'm tough." I told T.J. Sheehan over the phone. Thinking…I hadn't peed my pants that fateful day the grizzly walked my way.

"All right then. When can you get here?" Mr. Sheehan asks cheerfully through his thick southern accent.

"I'll have to check with my supervisor here." I said.

Rob, my supervisor tells me that if I want my job next summer then I need to finish the schedule. The Chief Paul School in Edinak agrees to wait for me but the question is will I be able to wait another ten days?!

I swing the naturalist's office door open and rush in interrupting Doug's lunch. There the wise man sits eating amongst the skins and skulls on the surrounding shelves of our gray office. Doug has the enthusiasm of an 18 year old with the wisdom of his 70 some years. His body is lean even though he continually passes out rice crispy treats so I assume that he eats them too. His clear blue eyes set deeply in strong brow bones and sharp cheek bones compliment his winning smile and a twinkle in his eyes.

"Just because you're gorgeously beautiful, intelligent, ravishing, wonderful goddess of the forest you think you can do whatever you want." He projects in his melodious, deep voice.

"Hi Doug, how are you?" I say gripping my hands together smiling.

"I'm well now that your shining smile is here," he says tilting his head grinning.

"I got a teaching job in Alaska with the Eunuchs!"

"The Eunuchs?" he asks scratching his head and furrowing his brow. "Do you know what a Eunuch is?" He continues.

"Well, I think that's what the principal said over the phone. He said he's been married to a Eunuch woman for twenty years and still doesn't speak a word of it."

"No, no…a Eunuch is someone who gets their…how do I put this delicately?"

"Oh I think I remember. They test the guards with dancers to see if they are…trustworthy."

"Yes, something like that," he says thoughtfully blinking slowly a few times, sort of like a bird does when they're relaxed and or in love.

"Well, I don't know if that's what he said or not but something like that. The connection wasn't very good. Well I'll find out when I get there." I put the radio in my belt flip for my afternoon hike and hurry out the door.

Tonight, I manage to convince my co-workers Lynn and Nicky to accompany me to Vera's for a beer to celebrate. Vera's is the local var for most of the employees in the area though most of the inhabitants are river guides and hotel employees with a few of the younger park service employees. Nicky and I are regulars in the small, friendly bar. Mostly to play pool which I have played terribly this whole summer except when I was playing Scott.

Tyler, the bartender always has good music, a friendly smile and remembers people's names. The darts are free and the tables and chairs are clean as well as the bathroom. On the natural wood walls are a map of Glacier and a couple of Charlie Russel cowboy prints. There is a neon sign in the window and a bench on the porch. For rock climbers you can try and crawl by way of the ceiling beams from in front of the bar back behind the bar to get a free bottle of whisky without the bartender noticing. I have only seen one failed attempt. Nicky goes back to Penn State tomorrow for her senior year. She's dressed up in a pastel floral, short dress and wears her wavy red, chin length hair down. I always tell her she has the best body.

"You're a nut!" is her regular reply in her husky laugh. Lynn is a graduate and looking for love like myself. All three of us check out the crowd inside before leaving the clear, star filled sky into the smoke, filled bar.

"Lynn is that Daniel?" I ask gripping her skinny, long forearm. She furrows her blond, expressive eyebrows and squints her eyes studying the six feet, shaggy blond man with sunflower, parachute pants and a purple t-shirt reading 'mad dog.'

"I think so," she says in her understated tone of voice. Daniel is leaning against the wood paneled walls next to the pool table holding a pool stick in both of his strong looking hands. Lynn knows Scott too and had seen his friend Daniel briefly last year like myself. Just last week after Scott left, Lynn and I had discussed our attraction to Daniel's visceral demeanor. I have wanted to see him again since last summer when I met him at a mutual friend's house.

Amy was the first to hear about him when I went to visit her in Moscow, Idaho last winter for a weekend. Felt great to take a drive from West Glacier to Moscow.

"Do you know Daniel, Scott Powell's friend?" I asked like I was telling a secret in a crowded room but it was just the two of us.

"No, I don't think I do. Why? Is he cute?"

"Yes, and really quiet. I met him at Ian's last summer. They were looking at the pictures from their trip to Asia with Scott. I kind of gravitated right next to Daniel on the couch which surprised me. The pictures looked like something from another planet with the yaks and barren slopes of snow. Daniel hadn't said one word since I got there. Not even hello but we held each other's eyes when I first got there. I was almost embarrassed. Then when we were looking at the pictures of Nepal, Daniel started singing the theme song for Star Wars. Dum, dum, da dum …da da dum da duh dum. That's exactly what the pictures looked like! Then the next day I saw him just before taking a boat trip outside the Many Glacier Hotel… He had on parachute pants with palm trees all over them. He was playing football with two little kids so I asked him if they were his kids. I figure he's 26. He might. He said they were his nephews and walked towards me across the grass. Then a very pretty blond woman walked towards him sort of suggestively. I looked over at her nervously but she was smiling at us.

"That's my sister." Daniel said also suggestively like he could read my mind.

"I see." Amy said smiling.

Now Daniel is at Vera's. Nicky and I sit down at the bar to order a beer to split. We wait at the busy bar when an empty glass is set down next to me with a beautiful hand attached to it and a muscular forearm. I look the rest of the way up his arm to face who I think is Daniel. His hair is a little shorter and his cheek bones look a little higher above his thick stubble.

"Are you Daniel?" I ask nervously but hopefully. He pauses, contemplating the question looking slightly suspicious.

"Yes," he says in a serious but soft, deep voice as he stares at me a little more suspiciously but says nothing.

"I'm Emmy, do you remember meeting me at Ian's last summer?" I ask turning to marvel at his serious, baby blue, sweet, intense, beautiful eyes. He pauses again staring as if he's computing.

"Yes," he says slightly nodding twice finally breaking his frozen position. I exhale. We both just stare until he gives me the run down on their rainy climbing trip in British Columbia. We exchange some pleasantries but I don't seem to evoke any interesting points with him.

"Do you want to see my pool stick trick?" Again, he pauses and I understand that his hesitation in answering questions is neither that of a paranoid mind or that of a slow mind but that of a strongly suspicious, very intellectual mind.

"Yes." Daniel succeeds quietly in Vera's bar that fateful first night spending time together.

Quickly I get the pool stick before he drifts away and take him, Lynn, Nicky and a few others who know the trick yet are still learning out to the front porch. I stand in the glow of the neon light from the bar window and look up to the sparkling stars quickly like I have a solo performance in The Big Apple at Times Square. Placing the pool stick behind me with my palms facing the small wonderful crowd I challenge them.

"Do you think I can get this pool stick from here to here," I let go with one hand and place the stick in front of my body regaining my grip again at thigh level, "without letting go?" I ask raising one eyebrow.

The generous gathering humors me shaking their heads no. So I hold on to the stick pulling it over my head to the front leaving my arms twisted while giving my shoulders a good stretch, then lean over pointing the left end of the stick through my legs, then (and this is where most people get stuck) step my left foot behind the portion of the stick that is between my legs. At this point I am stretching most of the muscles in my body which continue to lengthen as I pull the stick up my left knee, over my bowed head, down my back and legs which leaves me with one final left foot step behind the stick.

I stand up straight and proud like after a gymnastics event to salute the judge. In this case my beautiful audience crowned by the neon light behind them and the stars above them.

The pool stick is held firmly in my hands in front of me without any twists in my arms and without letting go.

That's the number one rule in belaying. Always hold the line. Never let go. "Are you ready?" Daniel would ask me. The correct answer is "Todo tiempo."

All the time. Even when his 190 pounds would carry my 130 pounds half way up the limestone cliff.

I look for Daniel's response while the rest cheer and laugh. Just barely a small smile grows on his half turned away face. This makes me smile. I smile even more when he tries. He gets pretty close. But not as close as he gets to my heart over the next ten days.

We cooked together in the Chief Ranger log house. Nestled above the cutbank down to the middle fork of the Flathead River. The two story, three bedroom house built for the Chief Ranger. But the Chief Ranger was living in Columbia Falls and all the other seasonal housing was full so I had the place to myself for most of the summer. The same one Scott found me in a couple weeks earlier. I felt a little scandalous because they were friends. But all's fair in love and war I suppose.

In the kitchen Daniel and I discussed philosophy and that we both liked Vincent Van Gogh's artwork very much. Daniel and I were pretty much always together except when I was at work but even then, he came to my evening programs to escort me safely home.

Visitors would flock around me to ask questions. And not that I ever felt scared. Just a little nervous especially at the Fish Creek Campground. It was the most remote and longest walk back to the park service vehicle over the bridge through the cedar forest…kept bear spray near but it was nice to have a man there protecting me just in case.

Daniel and I were bold in those first 10 days. Hardly knowing each other and attempting to Climb Mount Kinnerly. Next to Kintla Peak. One of the six over ten thousand feet.

It was an ambitious climb for just two days time. Camping out at Bowman Lake. Daniel told the other campers, "We're just taking a walk in the woods." I thought that was odd but strangely admirable and curious. Why didn't he want them to know we were going to try to climb the mountain we were all staring up at.

When we got off trail to the cliff area I start climbing up.

"You're messing me up." He said. So I climb back down. He liked to lead. But in time I discovered he sometimes liked to take the long way round. I preferred the more direct routes. Twitching my nose. Which way to go. It usually led up.

As our custome became, we ran out of enough food for my tastes but we did make it to the top of Kinnerly Peak. Was a little hairy and exposed near the top but I love climbing. And we did end up hiking out in the dark.

Bowman creek flowing pretty strong on our way back to our campsite. So Daniel instructs me to put our arms around each other's wastes and stand next to him downstream to ease the pressure from the water's beautiful, strong flow.

Once back at camp, I scarf down some peanut butter and ritz about midnight. The salt stings the roof of my mouth…so depleted of electrolytes. But slept like a baby that night. Something I usually don't do. Ever. A dizzy daze those first 10 days. Waltzing with Daniel.

"My parents said you can park your truck in their garage for the winter." Daniel offers a few days before I'm scheduled to fly to Alaska. So I do… feeling a little nervous watching the big white paint chipped door close my green Ford Ranger safely inside. But I know he'll be there when I get back. Safe and sound.

Chapter

The airplane will head north soaring over the Rocky Mountains. It departs from Seattle to arrive in Anchorage. Walking around in a much different kind of daze from the bathroom to the food stand I check my gate to see if it reads: Emmy go home. Instead, it reads: Anchorage on time. The headline on the newspaper stand is Princess Diana's death.

Daniel advised me to get a window seat on the east side of the plane so I can see The Rocky Mountain Range. I board the plane taking one deep breath and a final look around a somewhat familiar environment. This is good. I want to see Alaska. I want to teach. It feels like forever for the plane to take off.

Sunlight spreads over the mountain peaks and glaciers mirroring the Sun's magnificent light. I stare out giggling then all serious silenced by the pressure of the engines.

From Anchorage I fly to Bethel. Otherwise known as the armpit of Alaska. I'm stuck here tonight because of a storm. Weather permitting I'll get on a bush plane to Edinak tomorrow. It's the village next to the Bering Sea where I'm scheduled to teach fifth grade.

The taxi drives around town to a dingy gray house.

"This is where the teachers stay."

"Thank you." I pay seven dollars.

The owner of the inn is from California. She is creepy, quiet and large. Her son and daughter in law who got roped up here from LA interrupt my evening solitude. Packed in my three big bags are peanut butter, Ritz and cheese. I alternate combinations on the crackers when Corine, the daughter in law comes down to the hotel part and offers me to join them for dinner. I look strangely at the crackers, lick the buttery salt from my fingers and follow Corine and the pungent smell of trout upstairs.

After the awkward yet flavorful meal I approach their dishes. Coring shows me how to conserve the water as I look through the filmy kitchen window at the muddy, foggy town.

"You know I think it's good to take a break from the rest of the world," she says wiping off a chipped plate over the kitchen sink. Her pale eyes wide. Her bony hand moves quickly over and around the porcelain dish.

"You know, to get away from all the TV and competition," she goes on shaking her head emphatically, reassuring herself.

"I mean just for a year anyway."

I look over at her tall, skinny husband practically wiping his mother's nose. She sits perfectly still spilling over the sides of her throne at the head of the long, wood table. A dozen animal heads: deer, moose, eld, bear and wolf surround us on the walls. Looking back at Corine I try to smile reassuringly.

After dinner I venture for a walk along the meager river. The whole town is muddy and flat making the river and the land indistinguishable in sections. The salty smell in the air agrees with the humidity but the consistency of both is so strong. Much greater than along the Connecticut shore where I grew up. The chilly wind blows like wet sheets wrapping around sticking like needy ghosts.

The narrow, shallow, muddy river looks to be at low tide. It's littered with ragged fishing boats. Beater pickup trucks bounce by splashing more mud. A group of teenagers are hanging out a hundred yards ahead by an electrical shack with chipped forest green paint. The group watches me a little. They turn to talk to each other then look at me again. I pull my coat around more tightly. The collar's damp and cold from my hair tucked up inside. Corine told me the Eskimos in Bethel aren't racist but they're known to be a little more prejudice in Edinak.

The muddy road veers to the left away from the river towards the grocery/everything store. Boot scraping grates construct the stairs poking into the souls of my feet through the thick boots. The principal in Edinak told me I would need boots and not much else.

"The school has more than enough funding for any and all supplies you'll want." I don't know what I'll want except cereal here costs six dollars. Perusing the expensive shelves of spaghetti, sponges and crackers I shitter at the prices and abandon the food for the supplies and games department. The prices here aren't much better except for the movie rentals.

Daniel had helped me pack. Mostly he read 'Kubla Khan' periodically giving me suggestions based on his trip to Alaska. HE sat on the hard wood floor in between the dresser and desk leaning against the wall with his legs crossed at the ankles and his ruffled blond hair sticking out every which way. He nodded towards the sweater pile.

"I'd bring a lot of those. Do you know you're going where the sea freezes?" I raised my eyebrows stuffing in my dad's green, wool sweater. I was told the stores have potatoes and onions. Daniel's favorites but not mine.

On top of the sweaters, I packed the peanut butter, jelly, cheese and crackers. Daniel was slumping a little more staring beyond the poetry book. I stopped folding the quilt my grandmother made and knelt down.

"What's wrong?" I asked looking at his down cast eyes. In the last and first ten days in a row we had spent together he was usually looking me straight in the eyes. Sometimes they looked like a lion's. Brave, strong and sure and other times like the sweetest, most innocent and hopeful angel's eyes. Occasionally he had a hard look like the ice in the glaciers he loves.

He looked at me so sadly, "I feel like I did something wrong that you're leaving me and after we just met."

"What? I didn't know you when I took this job. I'm not leaving you. You're going to South America anyway. Maybe you can come to Edinak when your trip is done." I offered slowing down my words. Daniel smiled sheepishly. We looked at each other coyly discerning the expression of the other.

Any warmth I had felt is distinctly gone standing in a store with exorbitant prices. In bed I feel just as uncomfortable. I lie still on my back waiting for my heart to catch up with me. My breathing is constricted as if I'm on another planet and the small, tidy beige room is my astronaut suit. Each corner of the room is as irksome as the others with the white paneled ceiling tiles along a wood border. The narrow folding closet doors lead to no escape. The room door is also narrow with a seem of light at the bottom from the hall.

I'm the only occupant at the inn. Normally I write details about an interesting part of my day for a few pages. Tonight, I write:

8/31/97

I'm in Bethel, Alaska. The air is salty. Corine is nice with her pillow, cake and milk. I miss Daniel.

The threat of another storm passes by midafternoon. I call T.J. to tell him I'm going to be late.

"Okay thanks for calling. I'll be looking for you and be sure to get on Wayne's flight. He's the pilot that lives in Edinak."

The taxi drives in what feels like a circle to the airport. The sky is still dense with fog. We pass a few stores and frail building structures that look like apartment complexes. There's a thin layer of muck over every car, house and building. I begin to understand why they call Bethel the armpit of Alaska.

I approach the first counter of three spread around the airport terminal that consists of a fifty by thirty feet low ceiling and muddy tiled floor. Ten Eskimos sitting in plastic chairs continue talking softly or caring for their young children as I walk in. Shy, questioning glances are made in my direction. A few men are arranging boxes by the swinging doors leading to the runway. A young girl, maybe four leaning against the chair is smiling broadly at the men stacking boxes.

"He's so handsome," she almost sings to the tallest man with a mustache. He smiles sheepishly at the mother with her daughter.

"He's soooo handsome," the little girl sings again leaning and swinging from the row of chairs. His smile broadens slowly until he's beaming with the child. Their black hair shines with their smiles. The mother looks away shyly to my direction. Quickly she finds elsewhere to look.

I happen on the only other white person in the room. A man maybe twenty-five kisses a woman behind the desk. I miss Daniel. Waiting for about five minutes at the counter I pretend to concentrate on the safety instructions. Surely someone will acknowledge my existence. Finally, a man about forty comes out of the office with some papers that he straightens out and then looks at me straight on.

"Are you Emily?" he questions gruffly.

"Uh…yes."

"You're a teacher?"

"Well, I'm going to teach in Edinak.'

"You look like your twelve." He says matter of factly. I get that a lot.

"I'm twice that." I say trying to humor him, which works for the most part.

"Really." He chuckles shaking his head.

"The principal told me to fly with this airline. Do you have room?"

"Yes, but it won't be for another hour or so," he says flatly losing his humorous moment.

Wayne has a mustache like the 'handsome man.' I sit down behind the group of women with their small children and open "The Pearl" by John Steinbeck. I read the words of the first chapter but don't fall into the book until the second chapter.

"EMILY!" Wayne calls out. My head jerks up from the book towards the desk. My eyebrows raise and I meet Wayne's impatient glare. The women in front of me turn to look and then glance at my book before quickly turning away. The thin book feels heavy and warm in my hands.

"We're going." Wayne informs in a softer yet irritated voice. I look at my three heavy bags and cross-country skis. He walks out the swinging doors to the runway. I lug two bags out into the rain to the twelve, passenger aircraft and leave my least valuable bag inside for the moment.

All the women cluster under the wing of the plane. Most of them have spitted glasses from the rain. They huddle close against the cold air nodding compassionately to one another. I stand away like the omega wolf. Wayne looks the group over moving them around with small gestures from his hand I go into get my other bag. When I return my duffel bag is being crammed into the nose of the plane.

"You don't travel like a Yup'ik," Wayne grumbles.

A few of the larger ladies are already seated. I'm placed in the middle where I climb over two women. No one acknowledges our overload. The wind is picking up. There are lightning bolts off in the direction we are heading, probably fifteen miles away. The runway looks too short. The plane before us barely took off before the end of the runway.

All the women sit calmly. I try to make some eye contact but am unsuccessful with the first three women. The fourth woman gives me a look like she hopes we make it. It makes me feel better to interact but the calm expressions of the first three women were what I was hoping to see from everyone.

The propeller sputters a little as we wait to take off. They gust s of wind rock the plane. I pop a piece of gum but there's no safety pamphlet to read as part of my preflight ritual. I give a piece of gum to the woman who looked at me. Her smile is small but supportive.

The wind pushes against the plane as we accelerate down the runway. I hold my breath.

Slowly the nose raises up against the rain and wind like a skinny kid under a five hundred pounds bench press. I stare out the window as Bethel instantly disappears into the fog.

Nothing can be seen except the clouds against the glass. It feels like we've leveled off at a low altitude. I focus a steady, rhythmic breathing pattern until finally we break out of the clouds.

A view completely alien to any landscape I've seen. The principal said Edinak is on 300 feet of perma-frost. The propeller buzzes loudly and erratically spooking my nerves despite my attempts to zen out with focused breathing.

Chapter

Colors and shapes of an intestine stretch everywhere within my limited view from the plane flying maybe five hundred feet above sea level. Winding waterways travel east, west, north and south with no particular order. Like there's no gravity.

Water isn't coming together and then moving apart. The confused streams turn into bulging tributaries heading for a grander canal then turn sharply back separating into two narrow streams. The saturated land in between waters appears to be sinking as we fly farther out. A diarrhea spectrum of colors shade, the light brown tundra with a little puke green mixed in. It's all flat. This is not what I am expecting to see. No animals, houses, no trees, bushes, roads…just muddy bleakness.

The plane lands successfully on the short runway. IT appears it's the only man-made thing here. Wayne turns the plane with the prop sounding like a billion flies. Short gray houses come into view all clustered together. Maybe fifteen plywood houses on stilts. A few people de-board.

"Is this Edinak?" I ask the woman who took the gum.

"No. Two more stops." Great. I have to go up and down four more times, ears popping.

The plane lands at the second stop where four more people de-board. The plane now has comfortable sitting room. I slouch heavily into my seat as the woman with the gum de-boards. Slowly she gathers her bag over her shoulder and buttons her heavy coat.

"Next is Edinak," she says nodding with a sheltered smile.

"Thank you."

Wayne doesn't tell us how far it is. Fervently I peer out the window as the land appears and disappears through the clouds. The scenery remains strange. Wet and soft with muted colors. My forehead furrows discerning the black, shiny water moving through snake like waterways out to the Bering Sea. The remaining women glance peacefully out the window now and then but mostly look ahead in the manner of a Buddha. Their serene composure is envious and eerie.

After forty minutes the plane comes in sight of Edinak. It looks larger than the first two villages. There are two buildings the size of four semis lined up next to each other. There is an arched, wooden pedestrian bridge leading to one of the buildings. Boardwalks string the rest of the small one story-houses together. All of the houses make a circle with a field of tall grass in the center. The gras bends and waves form the wind we push against coming into our landing. It's about four PM. The Sun is low in the sky but still visible through the clouds. There's a touch of blue. I think of when my dad and I saw a shiny part on a cloud on an otherwise cloudy day years ago.

"So that's what they mean when they say look for the silver lining." I said to my dad. He looked at me sweetly perplexed and with in inquisitive smile.

"Look on that cloud." I continued as we both leaned over the fence resting our elbows criss-cross style on top the chain links.

"There is a silver lining on top of the gray where the Sun is shining through.

"Ooohh," he said leaning over the fence railing of the airport a little more and smiling even more.

There is a silver lining here too. At once the five thousand miles between my family and me hits like a truck.

Flying fast at the runway we touch down surprisingly gentle like my dad's landings in the Piper aircraft ~ just barely stopping before falling into one of the sewage ponds in the village. Slowly I step out of the plane standing in my big, new mud boots probably two sixes too big. The runway is a hardened mud. I look around hoping to spot the principal. There is one tall, white man with white hair waving to me with a big smile a hundred feet from the plane. I wave back with relief.

"You must be Emily," he says extending his hand. "I'm T.J. Sheehan."

"How are you?" I ask smiling back.

I expect him to say up to his elbows in alligators but he just smiles warmly and says he's fine. He studies my face a little. I do the same study of his round face with gray, curly hair, blue eyes with silver rimmed glasses. He nods again after his study of my face smiling at him. It' so good to see him again. So I nod too. He reminds me of Mr. Rogers but only no mustache and curly instead of long straight gray/white bangs. We both squint a little loading my bags into the cart attached to his all-terrain vehicle. There are seats for possibly four people on what I would describe as a dirt bike with four big wheels instead of two. Theis is the only means of motorized transportation on the boardwalks that are the only place for feet of wheels. The boardwalks lace carefully above the tundra, around the houses and over the streams.

My belongings fill the cart. The width of the ATV fills the width of the boardwalk. Not far from the landing strip, a couple girls start chasing after us waving and smiling.

"That's Jessica. She'll be one of your students." I feel my heart beam a little at the sound of 'my student.' Jessica keeps running until she tags the back of the vehicle laughing.

"That's the school across the bridge." T.J. Says politely over the sound of the motor. Not that he needs to point it out. Across the top of the huge aluminum, mostly blue barn shaped building reads, 'Chief Paul School.'

Behind it is another similar building but it's mostly red paint is chipping off unlike the spit and shine of the blue building. Both buildings fit the village as well as big wheels would on a Volkswagen Bug. Also surprising is that both buildings are held above the muddy tundra on stilts. Although the tilt on the red building makes it look like it's sinking. The schools are monstrous compared to the other small rectangular houses circling around the iridescent yellow and green tundra. The contrast between the pale houses and the rusty tundra clash but the natural wood color of the boardwalk and the gray sky balance the landscape.

"There are only two places left to rent. The one with Lilly for $400 split or the single one for $500. I'll take you to Lilly's first. T.J. instructs as we walk toward one of the other new white teacher's rental. She's a young mother with her one year old daughter that I'd talked to on the phone about sharing a house.

"This is the arctic entrance," T.J. instructs as we walk up the muddy stairs and into a room filled with rain coats, boots and buckets. Then he knocks on the next door. I'm beginning to feel like Alice in Wonderland and that the next door will lead me to another bigger door will lead me to another bigger door and another and another door leading to nowhere that I should be.

"Hi!" a woman resembling Alice says. She is a darling blond woman with her hair in a bun and curls cascading down with a matching adorable blond baby. They open the door that leads to a brown hallway. Between fatigue, hunger and the need to pee I have a hard time matching her enthusiasm. Holding her baby on one hip she uses her other hand to point out all the amenities like a real estate rep.

"Here's the phone. Me and my baby fight over hearing daddy's voice. Don't we Honey?" she coos tapping the tip of her daughter's nose. "You know I never thought I wanted to have kids but now I don't know what I'd do without my little girl."

"I wonder if I will have kids then seeing as I do want them," I say making her giggle and me grimace. Next, she shows me the kitchen where a pot of spaghetti is brewing amidst boxes of food and cleaning supplies. It's a tiled kitchen that looks like it came from the 70's – all brown and white. It has everything I'd expect to see in a kitchen plus a torturing like device against a wall with glad bags all over it. Lilly read my furrowed eyebrows and silence.

"That's a laundry machine. I don't know how to work it but it would be great to have with my baby's diapers.

"Hhmmm," I say more concerned than impressed with the strange piece of equipment taking up a large part of the kitchen.

"Can I use the bathroom?" I ask as politely as possible feeling the urgency of my full bladder.

"Well, have you heard about the honey buckets?" she asks escorting me down a little hallway off the kitchen. The bathroom consists of a bucket with a black glad bag in it with a brown, padded, vinyl toilet seat. It doesn't smell too badly with the half a dozen air-fresheners. Lilly has nice quilted toilet paper. My peeing makes a loud sound hitting the bottom of the bucket. If I didn't feel so dazed and hungry my usual modesty would have made me feel awkward but in present circumstances I could care less if a stranger can hear me pee. Sometimes it's nice to be tired and hungry —maybe feel some of the inhibition a wild animal feels.

Next is the last house available in the village. T.J. leaves my bags and the ATV at Lilly's reassuring me that the other available house is nearby. The boardwalks have become too narrow for two people to walk side by side on so I follow him at close enough distance to hear him muttering about which way to weave above the dark, murky tundra.

We make our way through the houses with fish hanging on lines mixed in with clothes drying. Children walk out on the steps to watch while I glimpse adults looking out the small, highly set, filmy windows.

Most likely luck is responsible for bringing us to the last available place to rent. In what little twilight is left, T.J. points to the door so I walk up the steps tripping a little. I pull forcefully and clumsily on the lock. Sophie walks around the corner with a scolding look on her face. My hand falls from the lock knocking it against the damp, plywood door. Sophie meets my eyes to say "that's better" as I back down the five stairs much more carefully than I went up. She leads me in without speaking until we're inside looking at the plywood room with pictures of a family on the living room's fluorescent yellow wall. Just what I need. Bright yellow. The color to provoke anxiety. She takes the family pictures down.

"These were from the last people." Nodding to her I wonder if she could also take down the bright, iridescent yellow wall. As I look around I'm brought back to childhood playing in the woods and making tree forts out of the same plywood as the Yup'ik's houses. This is three times as big but at least our plywood tree forts had old, shag carpets. My shoulder blades mince as I look at the furnace and wonder what winter will feel like in these thin, plywood walls.

There is one raggedy couch against the neon yellow wall and nothing against the opposing blue wall. The two bedrooms and kitchen are covered in plastic flowered table clothes and the light bulbs are burnt out. They honey bucket in the back partition doesn't have a padded seat. I decide to go to Lilly's.

"I thought you would." T.J. says softly in a unique combination of sweet and smug.

We wind our way back through the last of the twilight across the tundra giving me the first feeling of ease since I left Daniel and Glacier. Though it's a hollow sense of ease.

Shelly, the first-grade teacher is on her way to her steam hut. It looks like a short shed made with the natural, colored plywood. Although I wonder how long one of these steam huts lasts without paint on it in the ocean air.

"I just have to check the water. Would you like some stew?" Shelly asks.

"Sure," T. J. says happily. I nod enthusiastically. Shelly ducks into the small door maybe two by two feet in the middle of the wall. Once again, I feel like Alice in Wonderland chasing the rabbit. We wait all of ten seconds before she darts back out of the little door. I barley had time to wonder what she was doing before she invites us into her home.

Shelley's décor is eclectic but nothing past the seventies. She has a lot of crochet blankets and seventies beads that hang in the doorways. I can barely see her husband sitting on the couch through the beads but I can hear him strumming a guitar.

The room is brightly lighted compared to Sophie's one light bulb house for rent. The walls are covered with small frames with family pictures. The living room opens up to the kitchen and the smell of turkey from the stove. Shelly in her little fast moves like that of a first-grade teacher fills two bowls with soup and some large pieces of meat. I gobble the meat down and whatever salty broth was on the spoon. She watches with clasped hands. I think I ate the meal in a minute flat. I get up to clean my bowl with still a little broth. Shelly frowns at the food left in my bowl. T.J. lifts his bowl to his mouth. I smile at Shelly and then gulp down the warm broth. Cleaning my own dish makes her purse her lips a little so I stop and sit across from T.J. to follow his lead.

All I need do is sit and be served and then leave. Shelly walks us to the door.

"Come to the steam hut in a little while." Shelly says warmly. We make our way down the pliable wooden steps.

"Not bad for the first night —free dinner and a steam." T.J. says happily. "Have you steamed?"

"No but my wife loves to. We'll see you tomorrow."

I walk back up the other stairs where my bags are waiting. I drag them in through the first door past rubber raincoats, boots, garbage cans, nets, wood planks and other gear then through the second door where I can see Lilly cooking with her baby on her hip like my mom did with me.

I drag my bags along the brown carpet into the available bedroom with a waterbed. The sheets look messy underneath the brown bedspread. I pull out my sheets, blankets, quilt and down comforter. I lay them out with the bed cover underneath as padding on the dark brown, shag carpet making me miss the hard wood floor and the smell of the moist cedar forest where Daniel and I had slept. Now I smell the must of dirty carpet. Even so, I'm happy to have my covers laid out before I go to the steam. My bed of blankets is one familiar thing.

"Lilly, do you want to steam?"

"Oh no, I don't think I could do that."

"Why not?"

"Well…they're naked in there," she says making us both smile nervously at my bathing suit. Oh well. I'm all for saunas and it's a chilly night. With my twenty years old purple towel in rose designs I head in through the small door scraping my back on the top of the short doorway. The ladies are organizing their plastic basins, towels and soaps.

"Jergens bath and body wash is our favorite," Shelly says holding up the bottle. "Do you have this where you're from?"

"Uhh, yes but I haven't tried it.

"Maybe you could have your mom send you some and I could pay you for it," she suggests squirting a healthy dose on her washcloth. One of the other three Yup'ik women mumbles something in Yup'ik to the other younger woman next to her.

"You are a Gusuk." Shelly says. "That is what they are talking about." She nods to the other women but she doesn't give me the full definition of Gusuk. White woman, outsider, lanky girl or strange intruder. They smile slightly having been given away. I'm reminded of walking into an upperclassmen high school party when I was an awkward freshman.

All the women nonchalantly take their T-shirts and long skirts off from their crouched positions and head through the next two by two door to the steam room that thankfully is even darker than the dimly lit drying room.

"We're going to cook ourselves," Shelly reveals smiling. "White people can't take it so hot…can't stay in so long. It's too hard on your heart." I nod submissively yet feel a friendly challenge.

The plywood we sit on is wet and warm. There is a drop off and a barrel with small rocks nailed to the top on the other side of what feels like a steam cave. A rectangular bucket is attached to the front of the barrel with water in it. A soup can with a stick attached to it rests inside the bucket. Shelly reaches for the stick across the little drop off with her little hand and pours the almost boiling water into her small plastic basin to mix with the cool rainwater collected from the roof of her house. She has made hot water to dip her cloth into for washing her body. She dips the can back into the boiling water container for the next woman.

"Who wants to pour?" the youngest of the group asks.

"Eliza should pour. You're good at pouring," a woman close to my age says. All the woman's faces look serene in the dark – young and old, all their eyes are soft as Eliza slowly pours the water from the soup can onto the rocks on the barrel with the fire inside. Gradually filling the room with steam and heat. All the faces fading in a thick mist before the Sun reaches the horizon.

The precious chill quickly transforms into a heat that causes sweat to bead upon my face and shoulders then on my back. Eliza pours again bringing us into what they call the cooking phase. My heart feels like it's melting. My back feels like it's bubbling. The knots under my shoulder blades are dissolving. My elbows weigh down resting on my knees bent up against my chest. My head drops between my knees.

"Are you all right?" Shelly asks.

"…Yes…this feels wonderful," I say looking up.

"See we sweat out all the bacteria. Then… we wash." Eliza pours again. The heat is great now. I crawl back like a slug through the doorway to cool down in the changing room. The sweat is dripping from me like water after a shower.

I cool down alone and then go back in with the other ladies are still cooking themselves. Now Shelly takes a scratchy cloth, dips it in the hot water with soap and rubs hard on my back rocking me a little.

"You only get this treatment the first time."

"Thank you." With each scrub and push on my back Shelly melts the metal plate feeling in my chest. The hot rinse pours over my neck and down all of my back.

Quietly I make my way back to my bedroom after the two-hour steam. I lay my head down on my pillow feeling Daniel lying with me. Spooning me the way he did the first night except now more confidently. Again, I smell the moist cedars of Glacier. He squeezes me a little tighter inviting me into sleep.

My beat-up wristwatch wakes me with its 'beep, beep, beep." I press the button to silence the sound taking me from my dreams into the room that I'd forgotten falling asleep in. After a moments glance at the heavy dark furniture, I remember I'm in Edinak, the Bush of Alaska.

I sit up on the floor looking for my school clothes and tights that are still wrinkled form the voyage even though I laid them out last night. I feel a little like facing the day after braiding my hair and putting on my beige dress until I notice a stain near one of the buttons. Last task is to shovel down some Ritz with cheese and head out the door.

The wet wind turns my cheek. I squint towards the school and away from the sea. My chilled hands pull my coat tightly around me and then search my ripped pockets for gloves. A plastic bag filled with small, hard, round objects surprises my hand. Quickly I withdraw the hidden treasure for once hopeful instead of fearful of what I'll find in these bottomless pockets. Usually, the worst offender is a mildewed apple core. It's light and in plastic —how bad could it be? Watermelon jellybeans.

Descending the sagging stairs to the boardwalk sucking on one sweet jellybean makes me slightly encouraged for this unfamiliar morning. The school is a quarter mile away but taking in the setting around me along the way makes it feel longer.

A moody, light rests on the tundra. The water in the meandering channels looks dark and thick like oil. The view from the plane made the area look like an intestine. Lines of multicolored water running in all different directions twisting around each other. Now on the ground it's all tall grasses in oranges, tans and reds hiding the water ways. There's still a little green from summer but the air feels like the middle of the fast approaching fall. It all looks too wet to walk on. T.J. had told me to bring mud boots because they're on 300 feet of perma frost. Now I understand except for the surface of the ground. It's frozen year round so it doesn't have much draining potential.

"Don't go onto the tundra alone. Women can't go to the sea without men. It's bad luck for seal hunting. I'd like to go to the sea alone at least once. To witness it free of interruption with just my own thoughts. See where the driftwood for the steam baths arrives along Edinak's shores.

I can barely see what I think is the Bering Sea. It's a mile or so away while I walk over the biggest arched bridge in the middle of the village. The absence of houses here inspires me a moment to take a long and deep breathe of the rich sea air.

I make it up the mud grating stairs in these big boots. Lee, the secretary, who although is Yup'ik talks as fast as a Gusuk, possibly faster and ties his pens to the places they belong. He greets me with a rushed hello and shows me where to punch in with my time card.

"Go right down the hall and turn right, it's like a horseshoe. You'll see the classroom four doors down."

My stomach turns a little. I put on my beat up leather shoes that belonged to my mom. The walk seems long down the new school with new maroon carpet and beige walls with a maroon border half way up the wall. Florescent lights glare down on the hallway contrasting against the warm rising Sun on the tundra.

Donna, the fourth, grade teacher, who has half of the fifth graders unit I start, is already in the classroom scurrying around the room. Her long, thick, yellow braid looks greasy. Maybe she didn't steam last night or go to the school shower.

"Oh hi." She says in a nervous, high voice. Her eyes are wide and blink quickly like a bird's. Her long, denim dress accentuates her long, slender frame.

"Hello,' I say sounding just as nervous but excited about meeting my students.

"I'll just have you watch today and then you can introduce yourself to the class and the aides. This weekend we can switch classes and separate the grades." She says putting some papers on the desk.

Slowly the students file into the room looking me over without a word. A few give me a faint smile while others hardly look me in the eye. Donna gets their attention from the front of the room while I go to the back with the three Yup'ik aides. First they have their math lesson that goes somewhat smoothly. The three aides walk around the room helping students speaking in Yup'ik while Donna scratches numbers on the board as students blurt out problems. They ask the same question over and over without acknowledging the reasonable explanation that Donna gives them.

Donna asks who wants to get a woolly mammoth award for listening. A couple of the kids settle down for a few seconds as she races around passing out little tags to put up on the woolly mammoth bulletin board for a prize at the end of the month. The students snicker to each other after the teacher has passed them by.

"Cheeeap," one of the students says. A couple other boys chime in. 'Cheap. Cheap. Cheeap." Their deep voices multiplying like an orchestra of base instruments tuning, filling in the room.

"Okay, why don't we introduce the new fifth grade teacher, Miss Strauss," Donna says breaking out of the math lesson. I stand up and head to the front of the class with my best posture for a change.

"I would like to learn all of your names so if you'd please go around the room and say your names and your favorite animal. Then I'll repeat your name back to you so that I will remember."

The class seems to enjoy this taking their time to decide what their favorite animal is, which gives me time to focus on their face and memorize their name. I will have ten boys and five girls instead of ten total. The two to one boys to girls makes me wonder.

When I go to punch out, I ask Lee if my paper work from Michigan has arrived but it hasn't. I still wait to apply for Alaska certification. T.J. greets me on my way out.

"Do you have a minute? The board would like to meet our new teachers."

"Sure." T.J. gathers Donna and Lilly to lead us to a building adjacent to the school. This building looks older and a little more run down but still on stilts like the rest of the structures. Behind it sits the church with white walls and a cross on top. We enter the cold building to see ten people seated around a rectangular table. The ones with their backs to us keep their backs to us and the ones facing us don't look at us. They're all Yup'ik men. I look to T.J. to see if he will make eye contact with me which he does forcing a smile.

"Gentlemen, these are our new teachers. Donna is from Colorado, Emily is from Connecticut and Lilly here is a native Texan like myself so we'll both be talking with the same funny accent," he forces a chuckle.

The board neither turns their heads nor smiles with T.J.

T.J. recovers, "her husband is a pilot in Anchorage so she'll probably be visiting there a lot. Then T.J. introduces the board members to us. Without eye contact I can't remember who they are. Only one man nods when his name is said. He is a Saul.

Lilly and I head back to the place she is renting and the place I had slept last night. She talks on the phone to her husband for the reasonable hours that I could call Connecticut of Montana. Her baby cries keeping me up most of the night. I decide to move to Sophie's. The next day at school is the same with me watching as Donna battles with the students to listen and as I start to see to also get the Yup'ik aids to help instead of hurt. It seems wehenever Donna starts to get some control the aides interrupt her in Yup'ik leaving Conna in the dark. I'm not excited about having an aide but T.J. assures me I will need one plus Idon't have a choice.

Tonight, in the steam I get to talk with Sophie, my new landlord, who lives right next to me.

"Don't let anyone tell you to whistle at the Northern Lights." Sophie is one of the taller, thinner Yup'iks. Her eyelids are starting to drape down the way my grandma's did adding to her familiarity.

"Why shouldn't I whistle at the Northern Lights?" I ask half entranced by the steam rising off our bodies in her cooling room.

"Because they'll suck you up and take you away!" The other ladies smile so I do too ~ glad to know what to do. So far anything I have asked about life her is answered with, "you'll see."

"Where will we get our water in winter?" Now the rain drains off the roofs into big barrels outside of the houses. Then the water is taken inside in a smaller bucket to drink or use to wash. It's as clean and clear maybe even more than the mountain water I drink in Glacier. I don't have to worry about giardia here.

One of the ladies with short, curly hair offers me some perfume while we're drying off. "This is Carl's mom," Sophie informs.

"I'm the Avon lady," she says with a glint in her eye and the same dimples as Carl, one of the fifth graders. Opening her cloth bag she reveals dozens of small, shining, glass cosmetic bottles. At once I feel shy naked in front of one of my student's moms and obligated to buy something. Biting my lip I look into the bag in the dim light. The glass bottles flash in the bottom of the dark bag mixing giggles with clinking glass.

"She's just...kidding," Sophie soothes finding the expression.

Chapter

"Hello! It's a beautiful day in Rollins!" Daniel's father's standard cheery greeting is a song to my ears even with the broken connection.

"Hello, how are you?" I ask feeling my cheerfulness coming back.

"Fine, fine, fine! Is this the most beautiful girl in Alaska?"

"Well, this is Emmy in Alaska," I say refreshed by flattery and animation.

"Are you looking for my friend Dibanibel?" he asks in ib talk.

"Yes, is he there?"

"I'll go get him."

"Hello?" I hear Daniel's softer, shy voice through the receiver.

"Hi. How are you?" My heart does a little pitter patter.

"I'm well. How is the most beautiful girl in the Bush of Alaska?" he asks gently. I love how he narrows down his flattery.

"I'm getting adjusted. Can you hear me all right?" I ask. He's hard to hear over the breaks.

"Yes," he says and we pause. I'm starting to feel like I've had some wine.

"Last night I found out if you whistle at the northern lights, they will suck you up and take you away."

"Maybe you should and they'll take you to Montana."

"Maybe…but I haven't seen them yet. Do you know how they work?"

"There are storms on the Sun."

"Yes."

"And charged particles explode away from the Sun." Daniel continues.

"Ions?"

"Yes, and then the Earth's magnetic poles pull those ions or attract them to the North Pole and the South Pole. Then as the ions reach the atmosphere, they're excited and act like a florescent lamp showing us the Aurora Borealis."

"Very interesting. You did a good job explaining that."

"Maybe we are like magnets," he offers.

"I think we are. Do you think you'll make it up here?"

"Hhmmm…Maybe. I'd like to see you and the sea freeze. Not many people get to see the ocean freeze. Can you imagine that?"

"Not really. I bet it'll be pretty chunky. You need to escort me to the sea. I'm not allowed to go without a man so say the Yup'iks. I'll bring bad luck to their seal hunting if I do."

"Hhmmm," he says in an almost approving way. Hhmmm, I think.

Today in the teacher's office one of the Yup'ik teachers asks me if I'm married.

"No."

"Do you have any kids?"

"No."

He looks me hard in the face as he leans forward over the teacher's table.

"You're weird," he says backing away shaking his head. Another shorter man with a smooth face saunters into the teachers lounge, supply and shower area. One of his eyes is lazy as he looks at me not with the criticism of the teacher but with the curiosity of a friendly cat.

"You should come over for dinner tonight," he says the twinkle brightening in his eye. "I'm Harold. I do all the work around here."

A woman that I recognize as one of the aides walks behind him smiling a little with the same caring, mischievous look in her eyes.

"This is my wife, Patricia." I look to her to see if she wants me for dinner but she just nods towards Harold. That was interesting. I was accustomed to my mom arranging social activities. Harold and Patricia both look at me smiling.

"Thank you, that would be nice. What time?"

"We don't have time here. We're on Eskimo time." Patricia says smiling.

Before I go to Harold and Patricia's I go to Donna's house to see if I can start teaching tomorrow instead of waiting until the next week. Janet the other white woman not married to a Yup'ik is there with an angel food cake in her plump hands. Janet has taught here for ten years or more. Her thin, graying hair is in a Dutch boy hairdo. Her white husband, a high school teacher, is very thin and tall with similar hair only shorter. They are from Michigan. The sight of the cake makes my mouth water wondering where they got it.

"Do you think we could switch classrooms tomorrow?" I plead. Janet had mentioned to me earlier that her section of the fifth graders in her sixth grade class were getting restless especially Ruvim. He walks like a tall, stoic, warrior in a time of peace he's responsible for and doesn't want to lose. Most of the Yup'iks have soft, smooth skin but Ruvim's is so clean and smooth, even a Geisha girl would be envious. Janet raises her angel food cake to my request. Donna is outnumbered.

Making my way around the boardwalk I pass by a couple of students.

"Where are you going?" They ask as we stumble on some scattered plywood.

"To the Ardok's," I say happy to actually know where I'm going.

"Do you want us to show you the store?" They offer as a couple of children about five years old stroll out from behind a house to see what's going on. They smile sweetly studying my foreign face.

"Sure." I say peering around for a sign or a store to no avail.

"It' right here," Jessica says turning her head quickly in my direction flipping her long, silky ponytail. Looking I only see a plywood-looking house with mixed colored plywood propped against an opening. The two smaller children lead us in. To my surprise is a store with aisles of food, coolers of ice cream and a cash register in the corner. I gaze at the ice-cream bars then look at the prices. Five dollars for one ice-cream bar! I scan the aisles for a good deal. The best I find is on large containers of Crisco that take up a whole isle. The Oreos are six dollars! The people here say it's better to find a good catalog and order food from there but that it will take a while for the first shipment and getting it organized with timing. I don't know how long my peanut butter, jelly cheese and Ritz will last but these prices are brutal.

The cashier raises her chin a little and to the side avoiding eye contact with me in response to my smile to her. I swallow hard and follow the children back out to the boardwalk to the house Harold had pointed to out the school window.

"It's the big one with the big steam hut next to it." He had said the twinkle in his lazy eye gleaming brighter. He has a cute face more square than the other pronounced cheekbones on most of the Yup'iks and his Cheshire cat smile is fairly constant.

There is a white puppy outside the Ardoks tied to a short rope. He isn't much smaller than the other dogs tied around the village. His wagging tail gives his youth away. I put my hand under his chin followed by his ferocious licks. Scratching him under his chin makes him roll over on his back exposing his belly. He is the first dog I've been close to without being barked at here. I want to pick him up and hold him.

Friendly voices stream through the Ardoks door that is slightly ajar so I knock gently and wait in vain for someone to open the door some more. I take inventory of their big arctic entrance full of fishing equipment, yellow rain coats and pants. Real rain coats, not the water resistant kind but the thick, plastic coats. Patricia walks by on the phone as I peak in and she signals for me to come in. Her house is decorated similarly to Shelly's, the first grade teacher. Seventies, colored beads hang in between the kitchen and the living room. Muted tones of crocheted blankets cover the two couches perpendicular to each other arranged around the large TV in the corner. On the walls are bunches of family pictures in small frames. Both houses have a big picture of Jesus. It's the same picture of Jesus that is most familiar to me from church. My grandparents have the same picture on their walls. On the Ardok's living room window is the serenity prayer.

'God grant me the courage to change the things I can. The serenity to accept the things I cannot change and the wisdom to know the difference.'

This is my favorite prayer from my grandparent's house. My grandma had many prayers taped to bathroom windows, dressers and kitchen cabinets but the serenity prayer is the only that I memorized.

Patricia motions over to the hand-washing pan next to the kitchen counter as Harold comes down the hallway still with a little grin on his fifty some years old face. I rinse my hands in the standing water and lather up. The rinse water is the same, which is a little brown and cold. The towel is damp. I'd rather not have washed my hands. Patricia hangs up the phone and comes over to stir whatever is simmering on the stove spreading a dark, salty meat smell.

Gabe, their nine years old son and Leslie, their 18 years old daughter, stroll into the kitchen briefly for an introduction. I expect them to eat with us but they disappear as quietly as they had appeared down the dark hallway. Gabe doesn't resemble either Harold or Patricia but more a mix heritage with exquisite light brown eyes. Leslie looks very much like Harold except with younger skin and a high ponytail but the same slightly lazy eye and a constant, curious grin.

Patricia has me sit down at the table with a plastic, flowered tablecloth similar to Sophie's. Harold sits down across from me studying my face.

"You remind me of Jenny."

"She was a teacher here before you for a few years but then she got married and went away." Patricia says half sadly half in a fond memory.

"Are you a Christian?" Harold asks.

"Uh…yes."

"We are Christians. In the villages you never have to worry. A traveler can go from village to village and he knows he will be welcome. Even in the winter. There was a man who ran out of gas on his ski-do and we went out to help him." Harold continues in his low, slow voice with periodic inflections. His grin fades as he leans over the table in a light blue-collar shitt and a little wave in his short black hair. Patricia puts down a plate of dark meat, a bowl of corn and some pastries. Harold picks one up.

"I buy these in Bethel." The smile returns to his face. I try to eat slowly but I'm too hungry to use my best manners. Plus, Harold and Patricia seem pleased that I'm eating. They watch me for a little before they start on their own plates. They both smile when I lick the salty oil from my fingers.

At the end of the meal Patricia brings a bowl of what looks like ice cream from the refrigerator.

"This is akutaq ~ Eskimo ice cream." She says in her thik almost sultry yet not flirtatious voice. She piles a healthy portion out to each of us.

"Yup'ik women don't worry about their weight. I eat until I am full." She says smiling. She like most of the women here has a round body with thinner arms and legs. I suppose she would be considered overweight in my culture but the way Harold looks at her with pride and the content look in her eyes makes her shine with beauty as much as her black, long hair shines with health. She smiles in Harold's direction for an instance.

Secure admiration for each other beams from them. I wonder if Daniel and I will ever look at each other that way.

Morning comes quickly after the steam last night, which after a few steams all in different huts is becoming a regular part of my routine. More so than anything else. I watch how carefully the women wash themselves and am reminded of the seals that live sometimes a couple of miles away spending hours preening and cleaning themselves. So far I have spent a minimum of two hours steaming.

The night is sweet, warm and cleansing. The morning is sour, cold and scary. The Ritz package is almost gone as well as the peanut butter and cheese. The rain water from the bucket is soothing on my tongue and throat but cold on my hands and face. The thick, salty, cool air presses around me as I walk to school. It's another cloudy day in the village. Sun has not fully penetrated the clouds yet and I wonder about the dark winter days to come.

At school the students do anything but find their seats and prepare to learn. Donna is rushing around in her long, skinny body with fingers twisting around the room unsuccessfully trying to arrange some order. Jessica with her high ponytail is gazing out the window at the dark tundra. The Sun has still not fully risen at nearly nine A.M. Greeting the first student to greet me when I arrived in the village seems like a good idea. All I have to do is make it by Helen's suspicious scowl. Jessica looks sad as she studies the flat, dark and endless landscape. She glances up at me and then back to the tundra.

"Are there trees where you come from?" Her usually smiling face is relaxed and serious.

"Yes, so many I can't see the sky sometimes," I say trying to help her appreciate her home. Her face turns almost into an angry glare on the dark tundra as I glare at my miscalculation.

A I watch Donna struggle with the combined class I remind myself to call my mom after school. I need a care package. Before Leaving Glacier I had the joy of telling my parents the news about teaching in Alaska.

The night was the last night of my evening slide program about the Grizzlies of Glacier. A storm was building in the valley outside of the mountains giving an eerie, dark blue color to the sky with flashes of lightning that were coming closer. Only the wind had reached close to the heart of the mountains where the amphitheater was set. The grand cottonwood leaves were turning over and around blowing off the branches. The ten miles of Lake McDonald showed the waves growing to white caps. The Rocky Mountain peaks at the head of the lake seemed to grow taller and darker.

"With respect, we may continue to learn about the strength, the healing power and the warm heart of the grizzly. Thank you and explore carefully."

Heavy rain began to drop as the wind roared through the evergreens and cottonwoods. The audience darted back to their tents and I ducked into the government truck. Nobody wanted to hat that night. Lightning stirred the air and my body felt rushed and tingly with the electricity and yellow hue lighting the evening sky. Driving down next to the lake the white caps grew. I watched the clouds move in faster thatn the truck heading back to headquarters. The road was getting shiny with the start of the rain mixing up the oils. Faster than I could break a rabbit darted out. I felt the tire crush the small animal. I pulled over to move the rabbit out of the road. Just the day before on the same road I had run over a squirrel. Here I was a ranger to protect and preserve and I had killed two animals.

"You can't go to Alaska. You don't know what you're doing," my mom said. My dad backed her up. I'm starting to think she knew what she was saying.

"Mom, how are you?" I ask from the school phone.

"I'm a nervous wreck. I'm so worried about you. You're my little bitty bug and you're so far away."

"Please don't worry. Everyone here is very nice." I said.

"You're hard to hear on this connection." She said.

"It's just a little delayed. How is everything in Connecticut?"

"We're all just worried about you. Nobody can believe you're out there. You're four hours different from us."

"I know."

"Did you get your own phone yet?'

"No, I don't know if I want one if I can just use the school phone."

"You need a phone, Emily."

"Okay, okay but it probably won't be hooked up for a week. Uhh… Mom, do you think you could send me a little care package of food? The stores her are really expensive and I need a start until I get set up with a food mail service." I ask trying to sound nonchalant.

"You need food?!"

"No, no, I have food it would just be nice to get a care package is all."

"Emmy, what are you doing there?"

"I'm teaching."

"Well, what do you want me to send you?"

"Anything that can be sent. You know what I like," I say trying to make it easy which doesn't. I can't hide anything from her. I'm dying for milk. I feel like I could guzzle three gallons and eat five pounds of broccoli. I haven't seen a green vegetable anywhere in the village. One of the ladies my age at Shelly's steam brought me some donuts which were okay but didn't last very long. Harold and Patricia have invited me over again for dinner so I know I will be fed but I've never lived had to mouth before. I feel like a bum instead of a teacher.

Chapter

V

After school I set to work arranging the classroom. First thing is to go to the supply room to find the fifth grade books, which are all out of order but updated. I put the books from each subject on each student's desk to start. Then I begin to organize the room, which is in good condition with carpet, bright lights, new desks, dry erase board and big windows. It even has running water, which except for the water fountain part is turned off. Thankfully, the paper woolly mammoth on the wall goes with Donna. Besides the students tore up their stickers that were meant to stick on the mammoth.

The first thing I put on the wall was the American Flag so we can say The Pledge of Allegiance. Then I put the computer and teacher's desk in the back corner facing the class, which takes a lot of effort. Patricia told me to come over anytime but I watch the clock tick on to eight. Gathering my stuff and changing into mud boots I head over to the Ardok's with a tired back and an aching belly.

A few stars are peaking out through the low clouds on this chilly night. I wink at them for my class and to send to Daniel.

The Ardok's living room is well lit and warm compared to the cold night. Church music is playing quietly. Patricia walks by quickly looking a little sour.

"I wondered if you'd come."

"I'm sorry I was working at the school."

"Work shouldn't take so long. It's time for you to make some akutaq." Patricia takes out half a beach ball size metal bowl and puts it on the floor in between the couches next to a tub of Crisco.

"Roll up your sleeves." She dumps about five pounds of Crisco into the bowl.

"Whip that up," she says the authority in her voice turning into humor. I look around for a whisk brush or a blender.

"With your hand," she says in her sultry chuckle. Sitting down on the rug with my legs straddled, I start mixing up the Crisco but nothing is really happening except that the room is starting to fill with spectators. I look behind me from my sitting position. Leslie walks by slowly trying not to smile with a high ponytail and the back lower part of her head shaved to a stubble. She has a young man walking with her equally amused and unsuccessfully trying to hide it. They're holding hands.

"Keep whipping," Patricia needles on.

"I am." The room fills with smiles except for me. Now Gabe and Harold and Patricia's oldest son, Will start to watch. He is an aid at the school working on his degree. He looks serious but caring sa the only way I've seen him. The strong silent type. His shoulders are almost twice as broad as the other men's in the village. I feel a little embarrassed as I hunch over this large bowl whipping without results.

"Just use your fingers." Patricia says holding up her pointer and middle finger. Whip around the back and turn the bowl with your other hand. I start to get the hang of it as a few other people enter the Ardok's living room. Where are they coming from? Patricia adds more water which helps a little. Then she adds a little sugar, which slows up all my previous progress. I'm hot and my lower back hurts leaning over this huge bowl of white fat. Finally, after half an hour of whipping with eyes on me from all directions the Crisco resembles a whipped substance.

Patricia leans over with a bowl of the native black berries and pours them into the Crisco, sugar and water. I hope this mean I'm done. Patricia takes the bowl away and serves a cereal bowl size to the people in the room. Even though it wore me out I watch the faces to see if they like it. They all gobble it down and Patricia goes back for a second helping. She gives me a container of my creation to take home along with some dried fish, which so far, I like.

Walking home to my empty house is depressing to say the least but I am anxious to lie down on my bedding. No steam for me tonight but I resolve not to take a shower at the school while I'm here. Sophie said it takes up too much water in the winter. The men have to chop the ice up and put it on top of the school to melt. No more water off the roof during winter at my house.

"You should ask the other Gusuks to steam instead of showering." Sophie had told me in an almost pleading way. I did but no takers.

How will I get water in the winter? I lay my head down with cold bones having not steamed for the first time since my arrival in Edinak.

With no mirror I decide just to put on my glasses instead of messing around with my contacts before school. They don't go over well with the students and it's the first day Ingrid, my aid and Aaron's mom, and I have the class to ourselves.

"Where did you get glasses?" All the students ask as they straggle in and out of the classroom.

"I've had them since I was twelve but sometimes I wear contacts."

"You look funny in them," Helen says speaking her first words to me. So far she seems to resent me the most but her assessment of my glasses is probably accurate.

We start out the day with a math lesson that is still review for them whih goes well. They all seem proud of knowing their multiplication facts. Most of them do anyway.

"Miss Strauss, I need help," Lenny, the chubbiest and smiliest kid in the class keeps calling me over making me feel like school teacher in the Little Rascals and Lenny is Puggsly. He hasn't done any of the problems.

"What are you confused about?"

He just smiles at me looking me straight in the eyes leaning closer. I can't help but smile but I try to focus on the math. His shirt reads, "People who can't hunt work.'

Breakfast rime roles around so we all line up. I ask Ingrid how to ask if anyone is hungry in Yup'ik even though my Yup'ik makes the kids laugh but I figure I better try and learn their language even if they do know English. Ingrid smiles. She has kept an impressively stern expression in the class. I'm relieved to see her brighten up.

"Don't let them see any softness," she advised me earlier. I ask Sophie later what she thinks of that. She mulls it over for a little while.

"You don't have to be hard all the time."

Mark or his Yup'ik name: Passitngak is first in line studying my face.

Stalin, second in line shares Mark's surprisingly deep and husky voice. Stalin reaches up to my face and slides his fingers down my nose.

"You have a Gusuk nose." Aaron reaches around who has a higher yet still husky voice and mimics Stalin. Uncharacteristically not self-conscience, I turn and lead the line to breakfast.

The whole school squeezes down the hall way towards the gym where breakfast and lunch are served. I find out at this time that the aids cover the meals and I can go prepare. I hear a few of the students mumbling about Gusuk food in a foul tome. Pancakes and orange juice. It looks good to me but when I pick up the class I see most of the food ends up in the garbage.

Robert's dad, the third grade teacher who has been very supportive to me leans over. "Now they will really get hyper after all that starchy food."

"Oh great. Well, we have first recess after writing. Maybe they will burn it off then," I say trying to stay positive. Reflecting to myself about what Robert's dad said I realize I have to be careful about what I eat or I get on a sugar high but I never thought of how the kids would react to the food. Especially if their culture usually eats protein fro fish, ducks or moose.

Even so, I expect quiet concentration for their writing assignment for the day: "What did you do over the summer?" It's a typical assignment but insightful for me.

They all work hard on the assignment for their rough drafts which takes them into Sophies Yup'ik lesson. I go behind my desk and start reading through some good writing samples but I'm distracted by the change in the room when Sophie begins her lesson. Everyone sits up with their eyes focused on everything she says and picture she shows. Ingrid sits on the windowsill having time to arrange her long, crimped hair.

Sophie stands like a tree in front of the room, solemn and sure. The students reward her with reverence, poise and good listening skills. She practically whispers the lesson like a gentle wind blowing in summer. The students respond obediently. Only I cannot feel the wind back in the corner of the room. Two opposing winds come in like on the continental divide of the Rocky Mountains. The students squirm, throw paper airplanes and shout out against the rock lesson. A thought passes that there are hardly any rocks on the tundra.

After the lesson Ingird tells me, "We don't do science here." She handles the books carefully putting them back on the shelves like they have mold growing all over them.

Ingrid leads them out, as I stand defeated in the classroom wondering if the reding lesson will be allowed.

The fire alarm blares. We make our way down the harshly lit hallway. Red lights flashing. Stalin's deep voice, deeper than Vincent Price's voice is the first of many yelp/laughs heard filling the hallway. The students push and shove clambering out the door in mock fear as the teacher's try to quiet the frolicking mob.

We reach the boardwalk outside and line our classes up on the separate walks leading to different houses. When I count my students one is missing. I look all around frantically although I don't see or smell smoke. Helen appears walking towards us with her mom. Helen with the same tomboy haircut I had in fifth grade took the opportunity to go home. Her mom neither scolds me not apologizes. Just barely makes eye contact as she escorts Helen back to school. Through her big glasses and long face, Ingrid exchanges a smile of sympathy.

Recess isn't much more successful than any other part of the day which I was hoping it would be. Partly probably do to the gloomy day and the facility. I used to judge a school by its playground equipment. This school has a concrete court elevated above the tundra maybe half the size of a basketball court with a dilapidated wire fence around it ten feet high and that's it. I feel like a big rat in a box. A few kids get out and run towards the special education building adjacent to the school. So far I haven't seen any kids foin in or out of there. Just Lilly and Rich, the other white special education teacher. He is married to a Yup'ik woman who I hear sings very well in the church choir. Rich and his wife, Belinda have lived in Anchorage while he was serving in the military and she was working on her teacher certification and raining their two children.

Lilly and Rich say they're trying to get the room in order before they start working with the students.

Luckily, Clarence one of Harold's staff at the school instructs the escaped students to go back with a mere nod of his head towards the playground. I wish I had that effect. Clarence gives me a big smile as he walks by outside the fence. I smile as if to say thank you but I'm starting to see there's a two to one ratio males to females in the village with the adults as well as the children. I don't have a lock on my door or mace by my bed like I do anywhere else I've lived. Everyone knows where everyone lives. Not that anyone seems hostile or aggressive; I just don't want to be stupid.

For afternoon story time I pick, Island Of The Blue Dolphins to read. It's about a girl who survives on an island by herself. It's one of my favorites that my dad read to me. Except half way through the reading, Arie asks me, "Do you steal?"

"No," I respond respectfully to one of the first sincere questions a student has asked me.

"I thought white people are crazy and steal," Arie continues pushing her glasses up on her nose. The rest of the class looks up at me from their circle in quiet anticipation. Ingrid too looks intently at me through her big, dark rimmed glasses.

Reflecting on my own behavior and other stuff I witnessed…I can only say, "Sometimes but most people are good." A disappointed sigh falls from the class.

After school I ask Lee if my papers from Michigan have arrived so I can get on with my certification for Alaska and sign my contract. He is busy on the phone but he takes the time to look me in the eye with a sympathetic, "No, nothing has come in yet." I'm also hoping for a letter from Daniel or my family. I wonder if they're hiding my mail.

I took care of getting a phone but I still need to get a P.O. box. The phone turned out to be easy. I called the phone company, they asked me what the number was on the electrical box outside the house and they hooked me up. Sophie lent me a phone.

The post office is situated on its own, closest to the big canal on the south side of the village. It's made of plywood like everything else but with the U.S. Postal Service signet on the side. The only other thing close to it is the medical structure where I'd gotten my T.B. test for the second time this year. I forgot to bring the negative test results from Montana. Stalin's mom is the nurse. Her expression is sour with big bags under her eyes. She's slumped in her chair watching me.

I've been doing this for ten years," she says with a hard edge in her voice.

"Wow, that's a long time."

"Too long," she says forcefully pricking the TB test on my arm. Wincing I hope for a better reception from the post office.

The post master is cordial to the three people ahead of me in line. They finish so I walk up to the counter. The postmaster heads into the back for an extended period of time. Patiently I wait telling myself that she has something more pressing than a person. Deeper down I stat to understand why Terance Harris, the human resource personnel asked me if I'd been a minority before. That's only half of what he should've asked. Just because I've been a minority is social situations doesn't mean I've been a victim of prejudice. Sighing I start to miss mu post master in West Glacier.

The Edinak postmaster comes back out when the door jingles and she helps another Yup'ik. I wait as my blood starts to boil and reflections on history lessons about prejudice become a lot more meaningful.

I speak before she has a chance to walk away.

"Can I open a PO Box please?" She doesn't speak just hands me some paper work which I hill out as she disappears again.

"It's a dollar for the key," she says upon return. I pay and she puts the key with my number and receipt down on the table avoiding eye contact and touch. I look at my hand searching for disease.

Chapter

My students Gusuk names and brief character sketch are:
Trenton: shy but spiteful

Robert: teacher's pet with super long eyelashes

Carl: momma and daddy's boy

Mark & Mason: comedians

Helen: tomboy that openly hates me

Jessica: sweet heart

Lenny: large, sweet boy with a large crush on me

Ruth: wise and kind for her years and half Yup'ik/half Gusuk, willing to learn, very smart and so pretty

Joseph: class clown

Aaron: rebel

Arie: sweet, quiet girl that's kind of willing to learn from me

Stalin: a poet whose mouth gets him in trouble

Nina: also a sweet quiet girl

Ruvim: a big quiet and proud boy who is willing to give me a chance but not a very big chance.

Gives me something to start with in figuring out how to approach them.

T.J. had told me before I got to Edinak that they had plenty of money to buy supplies so I open the catalogs and start ordering. Some of the dids do't have pencils or erasers. We need art supplies I sign up for an art class through the television that Janet the sixth grade teacher recommends. Will

Ardok, whom I think they want me to marry is taking his college courses over the telephone. It seems to be working so we can try long distance classes too. I order red pens, bulletin board banners of encouragement and all kinds of paper: lined graphing, construction and manila. We need tape, staplers, glue, rulers and scissors. Most importantly are the composition books for each student. The student's need a safe place for their writing to keep and save all together for a portfolio to track progress.

I walk home with an aching stomach, my khaki skirt feeling a little looser today. A young man on the boardwalk is carrying a string of dead ducks. Maybe seven or eight ducks in one hand and his shotgun in the other. He looks like a glowing knight floating through the women and their chores. Their hands stop hanging and drying fish to look at the hunter approvingly. He smiles keeping his lips together walking tall and proud. The three look so content. My growling belly turns my thoughts wondering how long it takes laundry to dry in this overcast, cold and humid air.

Turning the corner to my house sinks my hope a little further. It has nothing hanging outside and inside there is nothing hanging on the bright yellow wall in the living room. The kitchen table has no fruit basket on it in its dark corner. All the cloths to protect the counters are folded up and placed beneath the sink that doesn't drain and doesn't run water. The only thing in the living room is a couch that I have covered with the pastel quilt my grandma made. I kiddy corner it so I can have the rest of the room to dance around in or exercise. I haven't danced in Edinak yet. Leslie told me it isn't allowed. She also told me playing cards isn't allowed so I hid them away. In the other corner of the living room against the blue wall is an accordian that looks fit for a fine parade. It was left behind in the storage room in the back corner of the rectangular house back to back with the honey pot room. Makes me wonder who left it but I'm glad since it's my only source of music besides singing. I eat my last bit of cheese slowly.

To think I wasn't going to bring any food. Daniel took me to the store to take what little food I did. Now I wish I'd filled a bag with food.

I hope the food my mom sent me arrives soon and Daniel's letters arrive tomorrow. My letters to him probably scared him away. Although he feared the same when he dropped me off at the airport. After just 10 days of dating even though we were with each other whenever I wasn't working, he opened up to me on the way to the airport. Way more than I expected.

"I like the idea of marrying you." He said softly as we were approaching the turn into the airport.

"Really?" I asked almost laughing. I looked from one bulletin board to the next along the highway.

"That would be nice," was all I could think of to say. We both smiled at each other nervously.

I was starting to get giddy from nerves and was full out laughing by the time we got to the airport.

"You think this is funny?" Daniel asked indignantly.

"No," I said hearing the hurt in his voice. "I'm just freaking out a little," I said trying to subdue my nervous laughter.

I'm not laughing now. I would love a hug from him. Just to be near him feels good. But to kiss the soft skin on his neck beneath his thick stubble is like nectar of a flower to a hummingbird.

My reverie is broken by the sound of a knock on the door followed by two of my students entering.

"Come in," They're already in. Ruth and Katie. Think they are both a beautiful mixture of Gusuk and Yup'ik heritage. Both of them are teased a bit because of this. They look happy to see me and even more happy to see the accordion.

"Go ahead and play it," I tell them still half surprised but glad they came over. Ruth is the first to try. Unsuccessfully. I let them experiment partly because I don't really know how and partly because I think it's good to experiment. Half of me thinks maybe I can teach them something out of the classroom if not in it.

"You do it!" Ruth says in her cheerful, brave and almost Gusuk sounding voice. I pusn and pull the accordion in and out pressing the keys to make some poor music.

"Oohhh, I get it." Jessica says. I hand it over. They all play it together. My ears start to hurt.

"Could you play it softer please?" They laugh gently putting it back in the corner.

"Do you like it here?" Ruth asks.

"Yes, but I get a little scared at night."

"Scared?" she asks almost in disbelief

"Yes." Surprised at her surprise.

"In church we're taught that it's a sin to fear." Ruth says with concern. "What do you do if you get scared?" I ask hopefully. Ruth pauses… "You just don't fear!"

Chapter

VII

"Hello?" he asks.

"Daniel?" It sounds like his gentle voice. Refreshing after the racket the kids made.

"Yes," he replies faster even over the delayed phone connection than the night I found him at the bar.

"How are you doing Miss Strauss?"

"Okay. How are you doing?"

"Pretty well, but I wish I was in Alaska with you."

"Really?" I ask with excitement.

"Yeah…I got a letter from you." He says in an almost cocky tone. Looking out the small, filmy window to the setting Sun over the sea ‑ I feel my cheeks turn the color of the crimson clouds. So far I have written one heart-pouring letter after another.

"You could come up here. We might have to pretend you were my cousin or some relative. They don't like unwed couples living together."

"I'd like to. I'm sure we could work something out," he says soothingly which makes me melt more. I feel that soft, warm buzz coming on again. His voice to my heart is like wine to my blood.

"Maybe I could come up in February after my trip to South America."

"That would be nice," I say but more feeling that I can't wait that long.

"Until then, do you think you could send me some of my teaching files and my magic carpet? My feet get cold walking around on the plywood floors."

…I think I can do that. You want your magic carpet, eh?"

Daniel has traveled to third world countries enough to know what I might be dealing with except that Edinak , but for a few modern conveniences is more like an intact, ancient civilization that is thriving than a third world country that by my standards is struggling. It's only the new, white teachers that are losing weight around here.

Next on my list to call are my parents. First, I hang my crystal from the window to cast some rainbows in the stark room. Unfortunately, it's too late for today. My first sunny afternoon in this western facing window.

"Hheeelo," my dad says in his usual positive yet business manner.

"Hi Dad!"

"Little Emm," I hear my mom pick up another receiver," Emmy?" she asks…mostly hope and a hint of panic in her voice.

"Dear, I picked up the phone first so I am going to talk to her and then you can talk to her," he says a little more forcefully than usual.

"Well don't take too long." She says matter of factly.

"How's Alaska and your kiddo's? my dad asks positively masking that he knows very well how it's going. He's just waiting for the straw to break my back and send me back to Connecticut.

"Well, they don't seem to want to learn from me."

"Hhmmm," he says.

"Do you have any suggestions?" I ask fanning through my Alaska Certification application.

"You know what's right for you. Are you accomplishing what you want there?" he asks leading me down the path of righteousness.

"Not yet but some of the other teachers say I need to five the kids more time to trust me. I'm not sure why they should though. I don't plan on being here more than a year. I came because it was the only job I could get from Glacier. So what was I supposed to do? Turn down a starting $34,000 dollar teaching job? How was I supposed to know they don't want outside teachers?!"

"You weren't."

"What am I supposed to do?"

"I don't see why you should live unhappily."

"It's only for a year."

"A year can change you." He says with compassion.

He's right I think I could be married to Harold and Patricia's son by January if it's a dark, cold winter and they continue to be my best friends, main source of food and they do have a gorgeous mink trimmed Yup'ik coat for me.

"Okay it's my turn," my mom interjects.

"Love you Dad."

"Love you too."

"Hi Mom, did you send me a care package?"

"What are you doing there?"

"I'm teaching."

"You told me the kids wouldn't listen to you."

"I know but maybe I need to give us more time."

"You are so determined."

"Well, you always say it takes me two weeks to adjust whenever I go somewhere. Right?"

"Yes, but you could get food in those places."

"I can get food here," I say thinking of the wide variety of onions and Crisco in the store. More thinking how gracious Harold and Patricia have been.

"Well then why are you calling me telling me you're hungry? Do you know how worried and helpless I feel? What if something happens to you out there. Who is looking after you?"

"The Ardoks are taking good care of me."

"Who are the Ardoks?"

They are the ones saving my butt.

"Harold and Patricia are a nice couple who work at the school." I say trying to calm her nerves. But I do see my mom's point. On the second day in the village I decided to go for a walk against others recommendations because you can sink in the tundra. Thankfully I only lost a shoe and not all of me. It's almost like the moors of England. I watched out for the fluorescent green patches on the tundra. Apparently they can be like quick sand. Nobody knew I went out there, not even Harold and Patricia. I was afraid a woman walking alone would also make them have a bad seal harvest.

"I know you. You're gonna get cooped up and go off exploring. Nothing better happen to you." She warns.

"I'm gonna go eat dinner, but I miss you. Think about coming to visit. You would like the steam baths. I love you."

"I love you too," her tough love voice metamorphoses into her sweet lullaby voice. She used to sing the prettiest lullabies. I wipe a tear from my cold cheek; check the furnace and head out the doors to the Ardoks.

"I wonder what she'll be cooking tonight? Ask the mostly white puppy tied up outside the Ardok's cozy home. His short, thick tail wags exuberantly while I hold the bottom of his jaw. That must mean it will be something good.

Leslie is home stirring the pot on the stove. She smiles inviting me over for a look. Duck's heads along with other duck parts are floating around amongst the stew. Leslie helps herself to a variety of duck parts. I mouse around trying to avoid the head but it keeps falling on the ladle. The feathers are still there. Finally, without looking too obvious I manage the most unidentifiable piece of meat to my plate. Leslie giggles a little. She has me all figured out.

"The head is the best part," she says slowly, challenging me with the same twinkle in her eye as her father. They're the two people I've seen that look the most alike in the village. Physically and temperamentally. Maybe she's right. The brown bears favor the eyes and brains of a fish. Maybe the same is true for ducks.

A loud commotion comes from the arctic entrance. Harold, Patricia and Will come in with dripping raincoats.

"Eeemmilyyy, you found our duck!" Harold says happily; my worry leaving me. "You never go hungry in Edinak. There is no need for money or the store. Let me show you."

Harold leads me outside. Patricia has gotten used to me looking to her for the go ahead so she smiles pulling her long hair out of the wet coat, shaking it off.

Harold and I go outside and cross a few muddy pieces of plywood making the bridge to his other house without windows. In the leftover daylight seeping through the open door I see a room with four white freezers. Harold slowly lifts one lid open as if he's revealing a sacred treasure chest. There are hundreds of big salmon. All four of the big freezers are filled with beautiful salmon. Ice crystals sticking to the fish glimmer in the little light left that hits them.

When we get back inside Harold is still glowing.

"What does your father do?" He asks.

"He's a veterinarian," I say turning their thoughtful faces into puzzled sweet faces across the kitchen table.

"He's an animal doctor mostly for dogs and cats," I say feeling the warmth of their kitchen. The smell of the dark meat still lingers.

"What do you eat then?" Harold asks with a concerned look washing over his face, "Ummm…cows, chickens, pigs and fish."

"So do you want to be a doctor too?" Patricia asks.

"No, I want to be a teacher. I used to help my dad giving dogs baths and cleaning kennels." I say remembering crawling into the cages with the lonely looking animals when I was a kid. Harold and Patricia look at each other in humored disbelief.

"What does you mom do?" Patricia asks.

"She raised my brother and me and now she takes care of the animal clinic business with my dad."

"Do they know who we are?" Harold asks me.

"Yes, I told them how nice you've been to me." I say except when I try to do the dishes Harold will ask me, "Don't you know how to be a guest?" I've retrained my years of being a good white guest into that of a good Yup'ik guest but it's difficult to let them be so nice without giving anything back.

"But do they know what Yup'ik means?" Harold asks leaning closer to me over the table. The friendly twinkle leaves his eye.

"No."

"It means the Real People. We are the Real People."

Chapter

I steam with the Ardok women tonight and get another back washing from Cathy, their oldest daughter while Patricia and her sister, Anastasia try to think of a Yup'ik name for me. Leslie pours the water over the rocks on the barrel with the washed up wood collected from the sea burning inside. Patricia and Anastasia talk in a soft, melodious chant in Yup'ik.

"Don't you wish you knew what they're saying?" Leslie asks turning away from the barrel. "Yes," I say honestly but too relaxed to feel motivated to try. Besides they sound so nice without knowing.

"We think your Yup'ik name should be for Anastasia's son. It's a name that means lots of energy, spirit and life." Patricia says solemnly. I lift my head quickly from my arms to look at the two sisters. The pain is heart breaking on Anastasia's face. Her eldest son's recent death while serving our country. He was the golden child of the village. I wasn't told how he died. His youngest brother, Cory in the fourth grade seems the most expressive about his hurting.

"It's the white people's fault!" Cory has barked at Donna and me. His brother having died while serving in the army.

I look back to Patricia and Anastasia's beautiful faces so close to mine in the warmth of the steam room. All cleaning together. Then I repeat my new Yup'ik name humbled by the honor and memory of Anastasia's son. Daveuk.

"Davauk… Daveuk" I say softly looking at Anastasia and Patricia back and forth slowly. "Daveuk." I say again softly bowing my head. "Thank you so much." It's a beautiful name. I feel a change my father spoke of. A good change.

Chapter

The Art of the Hair Spin

Carry, who will be leaving soon for college in Anchorage, exits through the small doorway into the cooling room to dress and go back to the house with Patricia and Anastasia. Leslie and I stay in the steam room. We're not as efficient as the older women.

The way they wash their hair is science and artistry along with some flexibility. They lean over in a crossed leg position and swirl their long hair in the plastic basin, then wash and rinse. The first rinse usually doesn't do the job so they dump the water off the edge of the plywood ledge from where we sit to go into the ground. Then they fill the basin with cold rain water from the big bucket in the cooling room with a soup can full of hot water from in front of the barrel where the fire is. Now there's warm water to rinse with. The drying technique is the most artful part. They gather their hair in a ponytail on top of their head, right next to their forehead rapidly moving their fingers up their scalp getting out any tangles. Then they whip their ponytail around with just the right frequency to give their hair a strong, full spin flinging the water off byt without moving their heads too much. Lastly, they swirl the ponytail into a tight bun right next to the center of their forehead.

Not all of the women I've seen do this because a few have short styles. Leslie is almost done with hers and watches me rinse probably checking if I can do it properly which I can't yet.

"Your ribs are sticking out." Leslie says poking my ribs gently. As a size six I would consider losing weight in Connecticut and in Edinak I'd like to gain some weight. I finish rinsing my hair and try to spin it out.

"I don't have a good figure here do I?"

"Will thinks it's all right." Leslie says slyly and cutely.

"What would Daniel think?" I ask like I'm a teenage girl too. And we're having fun talking about boys.

"He's a far away, what does he matter? It's going to be a cold winter."

"But I like Daniel."

"What is he like?" she asks flatly…protective of her brother.

"He's sweet, smart, strong…"

"What does he *look* like?" Leslie interrupts.

"He's six feet, strong shoulders, blond, shaggy looking hair, blue eyes…"

"Blondes have more fun, right? What is his nose like?"

"Uh…it's straight and narrow."

"Like yours? He has a Gusuk nose?"

"Yes…I guess…How would I say I like you in Yup'ik?" She tells me and I try to repeat her. "Assiken."

"No, Asick gum gin." She says emphasizing the ch making it more guttural.

"How about I love you?" I ask, the safety and warmth of the steam hut giving me courage.

"Are you going to say this to Daniel?"

"Maybe." I've never told a man I was romantically involved with that I loved him. Maybe through another language will be the best way.

"Ken ken ken," she says smiling sweetly her lazy eye gleaming. Which phonetically is spelled gin gum gin ~ all hard g sounds.

"Ken ken ken." I repeat to her. It's easier than maqiq – the word for steam bath.

"What do you call yourself?" I ask Leslie as she purs the boiling hot water onto the plywood we were sitting on and then squeegees it off for cleaning. Steam seeps through the door into the cooling room where I sit. The water she pores looks languid and graceful rolling on the dark, wet wood and then over the edge.

"Yup'ik or Eskimo," she states seeming to enjoy her task spilling the water over the wood. "What about Inuit?" I ask. She looks at me strangely but still with a mischievous smile.

"No, that's not who we are. We are Yup'iks."

"Okay," I say drying off.

Leslie hands me something that looks like sage she collected from the tundra.

"Suck on this," she says handing me a small piece. It tastes like sage.

"Should I swallow it?"

"No, just suck on it. It will help you relax or if you have a headache it can help that too." Leslie hands me a little more to take home.

"We should go on the tundra tomorrow and look for mice food."

Inside their house is a warm glow with the serenity prayer reflecting out to me. Quayana. Thank you. My heavy boots plodding along on the wooden walk way take me back to my dark house on the dark tundra in the dark night.

The morning comes on. I know, only because of the beeps on my wrist watch not because I see any sign of the Sun rising. It takes all my effort to push my comforter back along with the wool blanket I knitted my senior year of college. All square patches in mostly dark colors.

Today is my first Saturday here and I have to go to school for an in-service. Even though my stomach feels all caved in I limit the Ritz and peanut butter I eat to four and try to chew a little dried fish. I get through two swallows and put it back in the fridge with the akutaq (ice-cream).

The in-service is in the high school English classroom. This wing looks the same as the elementary wing. They gym separates the two. As usual I'm one of the last to arrive but I'm not late. Ingrid, the aid that's been my class motions for me to sit next to her. The rest of the staff is here. Of the nine white people, three are married to Yup'iks, two of them are men. Then there are we three women here on our own. Although Lilly has a husband in Anchorage. There is the older married couple from Michigan. Janet has been nice tome except when I was getting my room ready she told me, "Don't do too good of a job." All I was doing was taping a list of the class to the door. Janet's husband walks around like Ickabod Crane or like the old man at the bank who was trusted yet tonight was the night he was going to steal all the money. He never made eye contact. Supposedly one could retire comfortably after ten years of working in the Bush of Alaska. Lastly, there was the younger Ickabod Crane: tall, pale, thin, greasy blond hair. He was all ready to walk me home the first day after school. I didn't want him to know where I lived. At least now I have a pad lock on my door but I can't lock myself in. Sophie heard some kids running around in the house playing the accordion while I was gone. It cracked me up it was the noise that bothered them, not that they were in there.

Today we are lucky enough to have two visiting psychologists from Bethel to tell us how to manage our classrooms. Both women look pasty as do the rest of the white people in the room especially in the fluorescent light contrasting with the smooth light brown skin of the Yup'ik's. The two psychologists look wrinkled and outdated in their flared maroon skirt suits and long collared shirts. All the Yup'iks are in cotton T-shirts and long skirts except Ingrid the basketball player has on tight jeans. She is a tiny, spirited woman and keeps trying to get me to play basketball during open gym at night. It sounds like fun except that I'm too hungry and I want to conserve my energy.

"Okay, we want to set up some goals for the school and for the classroom," they say cheerfully sounding false and in a high pitch that is going to give me a headache. The women with dark hair start drawing a time line for the school year.

"Okay we want to brainstorm some long term and short term goals. Who has some ideas?" She looks out to the tired group of faces eagerly. Finally, the Yup'ik woman who teaches high school English speak up which is not a rarity for this fast taking Yup'ik lady. She sounds like a husky voiced Easterner.

"How about school team work and collaboration?"

"Great, great! What else? What other ideas? The room falls silent again and pretty much remains that way for the rest of their session except for her shrill voice.

I figure Ingrid will tell me later what she thinks are good goals for her son and the other kids. Somehow our visitors come up with some Gusuk orientated goals for the Yup'ik Village.

The long bleached blond with black roots steps up to bat to talk about conflict resolution in the classroom.

"Now I know when some of the kids have a problem they will turn their head slowly and silently away from the problem," she says mimicking what I've seen the kids do which successfully stops their antagonizer. It's something I also did to my mom in elementary school. She said it was the worst thing to do. Be passive aggressive and hide in my room but it worked.

The two phsychologists laughed at her imitation of the silent head turn but the Yup'iks didn't. I wondered what Connecticut teachers would do if two Yup'ik psychologists came to talk to them on a Saturday and laughed at them for trying to use 'I feel' sentences with each other to solve a problem.

"Instead, I want you all to put up a stop sign in your classrooms and teach a lesson on stopping, thinking, breathing, counting and talking it out," she says pausing between each verb finishing with a big grin. She must like to insult, criticize and impose on other people. It's hard for me to believe they have a legend about a white man who climbed the distant hill and started the winds blowing from what they see as their magic mountain. The location reminds me of a landscape in a Dahli painting, 'Visions of Eternity.' Just a slightly asymmetrical sharply, pointed hill way off in the back corner against an otherwise flat landscape. Of all the huge mountains I've seen this one strangely seems just as powerful but in a sly, isolated and elegant way.

I rush to the Ardok's after the stifling lecturer and take Leslie up on her mice hunting idea.

"Is that your raincoat?" she asks in a cute, sassy, put downy way. My dark green with big black triangular sections is my everything coat.

"Yes, it's warmer than it looks and it's water proof. Don't worry." But her frown is almost snotty. The day is just a little over cast, which is brighter than I've seen it most days. Maybe Leslie knows something I don't.

Leslie takes me past the old school that as we near it does look like it's sinking quite a bit. The sinking school. Now it takes up a good deal of space in the village like a dead elephant might in a living room. We make our way around staying on the boardwalk as long as we can but it ends sinking into the tundra. The glow of daylight ending makes the oranges, tans and yellows look phosphorescent with the water drops hanging on the blade's edges.

Leslie skillfully makes her way across the tundra finding all the firm spots so I follow her.

"Do you think it's boring here?"

"No." Survival mode is anything but boring.

"What would you be doing in Montana?"

"Probably hiking and looking for huckleberries. Not much different than here. Do you see any mice foot yet?" I have little idea what I'm looking for.

"No but here are some blackberries," she says picking a few off the two-inch high plant. I wonder what Daniel would say blackberries magical power is.

Hiking along Kintla Lake two weeks ago on my last day off, Daniel had instructed me on the magical powers of all the different berries in Glacier National Park.

"This one," he'd said stopping to pick off a red thimbleberry, kiss me and place the fragile berry into the palm of my hand, "makes you invisible so the grizzly bear won't eat you." I smiled and ate the tart berry.

"These," he said carefully picking off juicy huckleberries almost the size of blueberries," make you fall in love." Careful not to drop any, he nestled them in my curving palm. We ate them letting the sweet berries tickle our tongues. We looked both ways on the wooded trail by the lake to check for other hikers but I suppose it didn't matter since we were invisible and kissed wit our purple stained lips.

I wonder what he's doing now.

Leslie and I chow on blackberries for a while until she resumes her mice food hunt. She seems to be digging in the darker mossier areas so I try to do the same.

"What will they look like?" I ask half worried by what I might find.

"You'll see," she says with a smile that tells me she enjoys my ignorance.

"Are there any bears out here?" I'd wanted to go to Alaska to see the brown bears on Kodiak Island and thought maybe I could take a trip there one weekend.

"Sometimes at the dump we get a black bear. A few weeks ago, there was one there." I still haven't taken the long boardwalk out of town to see the dump but I have seen the ATV with five young men hanging on the cart behind it picking up the trash. Including the honey bucket contents out of the steel containers on the boardwalks.

I missed the bear. Although black bears are more predacious towards humans than grizzlies are. I'm glad I was instructed on how to behave with the grizzly on Logan Pass. Actually it seemed he was telling me to be still. It was his turf. I'm trying to listen the same here but it's harder to listen because I'm pretty sure they want me to marry if I stay and not to teach. I don't like to hear what I don't want to hear.

"Sometimes a moose will come hear the village but not very often." I felt badly for the moose trying to get around in deep snow in Glacier but the tundra would really be tiring.

"But the men usually go out and hunt for the moose before they get too close."

"Do you want to have kids?" Leslie asks rooting around in the spongy tundra.

"Yeah, I don't know when though." I say feeling that I'm still a kid.

"Mason and I are trying to have a baby," she says as if it's the natural time for her to start bearing children.

"Don't you want to finish high school first? You only have this year to go."

"Maybe. We've been trying for a while."

"Do you get your period?"

"Yes," she says waiting for more. For our 6 years age difference she does look more womanly and mature than me.

"Well, there's a time in the middle of your cycle that you're ovulating. That's when there's an egg ready to be fertilized inside you."

"How do you know when that time is?"

"Uhhh…your temperature goes up a little, you have more discharge and you feel more…uhh…"

"Horny?" Leslie asks laughing at me.

"Yes." Then she gets quiet so I leave her to her thoughts an tend to my need for food. Forget the mice food. There's a big blackberry section so I go over and chow some more. TI's hard to believe grizzlies in Glacier can gain fat off of berries. It looks like she might have found something gso I head back over.

"Here's a nest!" She says digging. She gets to the bottom of the spot that does look like an animal had shelter but it's empty.

"There have to be more nearby," shew says and starts digging another spot.

"How many people are in Edinak?" I ask

"About six hundred." The Yup'iks and Daniel are both good at either avoiding a question or not elaborating.

"How many people when you were born?"

"About three hundred," she says stopping to look towards the village. "Too much fucking." We both giggle. Damn. Another empty nest.

"Do you want to see our graveyard?" she asks. "Sure."

Making our way across the tundra tuns out to be time consuming but my boots are keeping my feet dry. We reach the fenced in graveyard maybe thirty feet squared and isolated half a mile from the village and boardwalks close to sunset. There's still enough daylight to read the wooden grave sights. Leslie walks around looking for her relatives. Both of us gingerly step over where the bodies are buried. It's tight because they are buried close together. Some of the grave sights are knocked over or the plastic flowers are at one end and the wooden cross is at the other end. I can't tell where the head is. It's like we both start falling over hollow egg and are trying not to crack them but they start multiplying as we move faster.

We make a dash for the perimeter on opposite sides and walk slowly around towards the other. A strange feeling like a cold wind blowing into my sternum and out my stomach moves through me. Leslie must feel the same thing, because we run for the gateway. Out of the graveyard. The ground squishes down pulling our feet trying to hold our attempt to flee. I fall on my hands splashing mud up on my face and glasses.

"We both got spooked out at the same time." Leslie says half scared half laughing.

"Yeah we did. That was weird. I don't think they wanted us there." I say futilely wiping my glasses off for the rain drops to speckle up again.

Still spooked we walk up to the arctic entrance of the Ardok's house where the friendly, mostly white puppy is lying on his side whimpering. The puppy's leg is visibly twisted and broken even with the white cloth around the broken front leg. I bend down to inspect and maybe soothe but that only makes the puppy try to get away so I back off.

"How should we kill it?" Leslie's boyfriend asks. He has a bat in his hand. I say nothing for the time being. The puppy like on towels surrounded by a wet raincoat. A severely pained expression shows in his dark eyes looking up at us like vultures. Patricia walks up wet from fishing.

"Who did this?" she asks glaring at the puppy and then me.

"I didn't do it," I defend instantly fearing the loss of their hospitality. She marches into the house and then back out again a little calmer. Earlier I caught her giggling to her oldest daughter that I used to bathe dogs like it was the silliest thing she'd ever heard. I can see why she suspects me of not only bringing the puppy into the house but also bandaging his leg. Patricia sighs at me sympathizing with the puppy.

"Oh just leave it," she sighs. Gabe, her fourth grader brings the puppy some food and water. Patricia sends Leslie home with me to teach how to clean and prepare the fish they give. Two fresh whitefish and one frozen salmon.

It' nearing ten o'clock Montana time but I decide to call Daniel.

"Hello, it's a beautiful day in Rollins," his dad says bringing a smile to my face.

"Hello, is Daniel there?"

"No, actually he went for a bike ride to Hot Springs."

"Oh *geez,*" I say knowing it's fifty miles from their house and it's dark there now and will be for the next twelve hours.

"Oh geez is right." His dad says.

"Well, could you tell him I called please?" I ask giving him my number. I hang up hoping he wont get hurt riding on the two lane highway with occasional semis driving in the middle of the night.

From my couch I hear the door open behind me. It's Sophie looking ready for a steam. It's that time of night. Eight o'clock.

"Do you want to steam?" I drop the letter I'm composing.

"Yes" I say standing up. I grab my purple towel. Sophie looks around at the sparse house she's renting to me probably wondering what I did with all the plastic tablecloths.

"Don't you have a wash cloth or a basin?" Sophie asks almost alarmed.

"No, I just brought this towel." I say wondering if that's why people keep offering to wash my back…and if that's the case I don't want a washcloth.

"I'll get you one," she says hurrying out the door. She comes back in record time from next door. We head out into the cold with the glow of house lights through the small windows. They light our way to the other side of the village. A new steam hut. I feel like a steam hut slut and I love every one of them.

When we get there Sophie makes some quick and quiet introductions. We are a little late.

Sophie and I crawl into the steam room after the other two women are already in mid cook. The heat enters every pore on my body changing the chill to a sweat instantly. They pour more water on the rocks and speak softly to each other in ancient sounds like a sacred prayer. Sophie looks to me to see if I'm okay in the hot temperature.

"You take it hotter than most Gusuks," the hostess says almost as a concerned warning. Other steam huts have told me to be careful of my heart. But I don't' know if anything could be better. It beats slowly now. Beating like a faithful heart. Or maybe like a bear's heart in its winter sleep. My breathing deepens too. The heat makes me full and heavy with prickle on my back. My breathing slows almost to a stop. I crawl into the cooling room. The other women follow.

We all sit quietly cooling down gazing at different corners of the three-foot high room. The soft, deep sounds of the ladies voices are as soothing as the steam. Linguists say you gain another soul when you learn another language. Sounds like these ladies have a soul from a land far from mine.

Theirs is peaceful and rhythmic. Speaking to worship instead of debate of banter. Just a low stream of sound echoing off each other. A sharing of spirits not of minds, hearts not of convictions. A choreograph of consolation cultivated for thousands of years.

Wind enters through the hinge. They stop. My eyes open. They're all staring at me. A fly is buzzing around by the twenty-watt light bulb.

"Live music," Sophie laughs…softly. On our walk home Sophie stops.

"I forgot my glasses!" She proclaims in disbelief. The steam has a soothing way of making me forget too.

Through the night though after I've cooled down my dreams help me remember. I wake to dreams of high school friends and my brother and I playing can't touch the ground in the basement and my mom and dad in the kitchen with the delicious smell of pot roast in the oven. The dreams are so vivid they wake me as if from a nightmare.

Still I manage to sleep in on this dreary Sunday morning. Church doesn't start until 10:00 AM. The Ardoks asked me to go with them, which I'm happy to do. I miss the church I grew up in. My bones feel a little e like a hollow birds and my muscles feel like they are shrinking after a week of minimal exercise but I make my way up from the floor to my dresser. It looks so plain. Only one of my framed pictures of my family made the journey.

The injured puppy outside the Ardok's looks like he's in a little less pain and fear but still hasn't left the arctic entrance. Harold and Patricia greet me at the door all ready for church. We enter the little white church with a steeple and Cross. They seat me in-between them just like my parents do. I'm the only Gusuk among them. Robert's dad smiles from the choir to greet me as others nod approvingly.

The sermon alternates from Yup'ik to English so I can say the Lord's Prayer with them. Harold glances in my direction smiling that I know it and recite it with them softly by heart. The organ begins an unfamiliar tune followed by a high-pitched song. The singing is a strange and unexpected switch from the Yup'ik's deep speaking voices. One of my student's aunts and the special education teacher's wife stands up to sing a solo. Her long, black hair has waves flowing down along her make up face and streams down her arms. She sings ochapelo reminding me of Whitney Houston filling the church with her voice. She overflows the church with her singing. People start moving around in their seats uncomfortably. I'm moved by her beautiful singing. The rest of the congregation seems disgruntled.

"She's too loud," one of the first elderly people I've seen in the village says to Patricia after the service. Ingrid is the next to greet us smiling wholeheartedly. Many other people patting me on the arm or saying hello follow her. Now I know how the people feel at my church who wear the pink visitor name tags around the punch and donuts after the service. It's nice though. Patricia helps me make my way out the door.

"Laura's birthday is today. Are you hungry?" I've been is a state of perpetual hunger for almost a week.

"Yes" I say enthusiastically. Harold smiles. My suspicion grows that they're trying to fatten me up for their son, Will. But I correct myself and know they're happy I have a healthy appetite.

"Laura's house is one of the closest to the post office. Where I've been stalking for packages of Daniel's letters. There's a line of people going into the birthday girl's house and a line going out. The whole village through the course of the day will have gone in, wished the child a happy day and feasted from rich food that her family has prepared.

There's a long table in the living room that people are sitting at eating peacefully while other people stand around the room also enjoying their meal. I feel my Connecticut roots surfacing as I push my way through the crowd trying to find the food. Everyone seems tolerant of me, which makes me slow down a little. At least until I reach the kitchen and find that it's full of platters and dishes of freshly cooked game, Jell-O salads and cakes.

I find a plate and take a little of everything. Dark meats, light meats, fish, biscuits and cake. I don't know what half of the meats are but they melt in my mouth. A spot opens up next to Beatrice on the couch so I take a seat. She moved here twelve years ago and although her roots are Gusuk, she sounds like a Yup'ik, which irritates me. The slow Yup'ik infelctions don't sound right coming out of her Gusuk mouth with her Gusuk nose and pretty hazel eyes. I feel badly that her accent irritates me since she has lived here so long.

"How are you doing?" she asks kindly which makes me feel like a jerk.

"I don't know…how do you think I'm doing?" I ask sincerely.

"Well, you're eating the mink. I'd say you're doing pretty well." Beatrice says.

"Is that what this is? It's really good," I say gulping it down. Then I ask her, "Do you have any advice for me?"

Beatrice breathes in a moment and exhales weighing the question and my posture.

"Just sit back and relax," she says slumping farther into the old couch. I'm going to sit back and eat. A few of the women give me funny looks that are arranging the food when I go up for thirds. I wish Laura a happy ninth birthday. She looks so happy and sweet. Laura flits around the room in her blue dress with a big white bow. Twirling, dancing and bowing as she goes.

Chapter

Today is Sunday. It's my day of rest. But it's cut short because of lesson plans. I wonder if Ingrid will approve. I'm hopeful because I work out recess to be after meal times, gym class to be at the end of the day when they get the antsiest and the academics to be after of before digestion times for the students as well as myself. Today makes for my first food coma since my arrival. Finding a food catalogue is turning out to be a wild goose chase.

The lesson I'm most hopeful about is the art/motivational lesson. The students will make a bulletin board with their handprints, names and designs with 'Teamwork' above it so they can see I'm on their side. So far Ingrid's pizza party point board hasn't been motivational towards good behavior. The students just keep putting up their own checks towards their goal of twenty checks, which makes them end up losing their checks and tuning the class into a civil war between the girls (minus Helen) and Robert and the rest of the boys. Robert has been brave as the only boy willing really want to learn from me.

"C'mon guys, be good. I want to learn here," he says when paper airplanes are thrown or check marks are made by the students on the pizza board. Robert's dad, the third grade teacher, has also been encouraging me at the end of the day.

"Well, they're a lot quieter now. I can't hear them through the walls anymore." He says in a sweet fatherly tone.

"That's something, I guess." I say rolling my eyes.

"If you can manage them that's half the battle," he says kindly with the same big, dark, encouraging eyes as his son, Robert. Even so my chin falls to my sighing chest. My heartbeat telling me to get real is getting louder. I don't want to be a manager. I want to be a teacher.

I also set up a pen-pal program with a friend who teaches in Michigan and a research project on the different states in America. Each student chooses which state they want. The library has a good selection of resources on the topic.

The walk home from school is peaceful but lonely. All the houses have fish hanging out to dry and people walking in and out. I decide to take the long way back so I can see out towards the ocean without sa many houses in the way. Only the horizon of where the ocean starts is visible to me from my sunken position on the boardwalk.

"Emily," Anastasia's husband calls from his outside stairs. I didn't know they lived here next to the biggest canal. The tide is low now exposing the muddy banks.

"Hello," I say straightening up to the head of the board of trustees and for his deceased son who I've been renamed for.

"Are you hungry?" My body must have been so hungry that it went into overdrive digesting the birthday food. Six hours later I again feel like a piece of grass waving in the tundra.

"Yes."

"Come in we're about to eat," he says looking tall and distinguished. His hair is kind of long around his face like Daniel's only black instead of blond. Once again the man does the inviting and I fear Anastasia wont like that but I'm starting to learn that's the way things are here.

Their house is a lot like the other's homes except that it has higher ceilings and looks messier. Maybe the way a house would look if its heart were broken by the death of their son.

Cory, their fourth grader glances at me quickly then back to his cartoons. Cory shares the same proud look and buzz cut that Ruvim in my class has.

"You picked a good night to walk by. We're having herring," the father says brightly. I start to feel his strength in keeping his family from sinking under their loss. Cory, who is a difficult student looks shy now but gives me another quick glance. This time he's smiling a little so I sit and watch cartoons with him sinking deeply into the couch covered by a mustard colored sheet.

We sit as rigidly as possible glancing at each other every once in a while to smile about the cartoons. Mostly we enjoy watching Road Runner foiling the Wily Coyote.

Finally Anastasi comes in from the back of the house. She, like her sister Patricia, has a warm lasting and sincere smile that soothes and impresses me.

"When is my pizza ready?" Cory asks.

"Oh when I heat it up," she says to him and then to me, "Kids are loosing their culture eating the Gusuk food." Her warm smile turns down sadly. She goes to heat up the pizza returning with a spot of sauce on her long, loose skirt and T-shirt.

"Shoot! Shoot!" she says loudly enough to half resemble a yell.

"Don't yell," her husband tells her gently and then to me, "like she can't wash the skirt."

"He doesn't like me to yell," she says smiling again caressing Cory on the cheek. I haven't seen an adult get directly angry at one child. Ingrid calls out orders in the classroom but more like a general than a hot tempered woman.

Cory has his dinner so now it's time for the adults. Anastasia's other sister and her husband come over to eat.. They look a little older especially Anastasia's brother in law but they're both quiet as they peacefully take two seats next to each other at the smaller table. Anastasia and her husband sit across from me at the bigger table perpendicular to the smaller one. Only the television Cory is watching can be heard as Anastasia serves the herring frist to me, then to her sister and brother in laws. Then to her husband and herself.

"This is a delicacy but you don't want to eat too much or it might make you sick. It's so rich and you're not used to it," Anastasia's husband advises me. The oil tastes as thick as gasoline but it's sweet. I peer up to Anastasia's sister. Her black hair in a disheveled yet graceful bun and her cheekbones are as prominent as a whale's back. She holds the shiny black meat with her fingers. Oil runs down her hands. She licks them clean and then bites the meat again. She stares back at me with the power of a content tiger and the grace of a queen.

Anastasia and her husband watch me seemingly surprised by my appetite.

"That's enough for you," her husband tells me. So I start to clear my plate.

"Don't you know how to be a guest?" he asks almost raising his voice. I sit back down watching them finish the meal wishing I knew how to sit still more comfortably.

Satiated after the dinner I stop on top of the arched bridge outside Anastasia's house. The water level is rising below me in the canal. A pretty red glow is spreading over the tundra, canals and hoses next to the bay leading to the Bering Sea. The wind moves the clouds across the sky and me back to my home.

The wind grows stronger as I enter the house. It sucks the door in closing it tightly behind me. I'm swallowed into this cold house devoid of charms and comforts except the heater thankfully and the couch with my grandmother's quilt. The bright yellow wall strips the soft colors that I fall down on.

A piercing ring startles me from my reclined position. I struggle to untangle myself from the quilt and reach for the phone.

"Hello?"

"Hello," the voice says demurely giving Daniel away.

"Daniel?"

"Yes?"

"How was Hot Springs?"

"Good."

"Good?" I ask hoping he'll elaborate on a place that we romanced in. The hot springs of Hot Springs, Montana. The free pool because it's on tribal land. Daniel and I had the pool to our ourselves one evening looking out across the plans to the rolling hills and then the mountains.

"It was nice, but I wished you were with me.

"Me too…oh geez," I say looking out the window at the boardwalk.

"Two of my students are swinging an injured seagull. Each has a wing in their hand and they're swinging the seagull back and forth like my parents used to do to me…holding my hands. Which I loved. But pretty sure the seagull does not feel the same.

"Boys will be boys," Daniel says.

"Oh the poor bird," I say turning my head away from the window.

"Have you seen anybody playing the drums in the village?"

"Hmm, no I don't think they have music here except in church. Dancing isn't allowed."

"That's strange. I thought they played some kind of drum there."

"I don't know but I did learn some Yup'ik. Do you know what…ken ken ken means?" I ask shyly.

"Ken…ken…ken?" je repeats slowly.

"Yes that was right. It means I love you."

"…Ken…ken…ken…" He says again softly.

"Ken, ken, ken," I say relieved and inspired by his response dropping back into the couch.

"Do you think you'll make it up here? They do commercial fishing here if you don't feel comfortable about hunting seals. I saw a neat old fishing boat marooned next to the bay. It had a red captains pilot box place and a white hull with a black stripe. It looked like a good boat at one time. Also like a good model for a Van Gogh painting."

"I think that would be pretty cool to see the sea freeze but I told my brother I would climb Aconcogua with him in January. I'd also like to be with you now but my mom made all these plans for us in South America… we'll figure something out."

"I would go with your family if I were you. I don't know what you'd do up here now. Besides I'm at school a lot."

"I'm pretty good at finding things to do… I could paint, read, play the guitar ~ or write you love poems while you're teaching. Besides, you're done at three right?"

"Well, the kids are done at three but I hope that's just because I'm getting everything organized."

"That doesn't seem right."

"No, a lot of things don't seem right tome. Maybe I'll be back in Montana before you know it."

"Don't do that."

"Why not?"

"Well, don't you want to teach?"

"Yes but they don't want white teachers unless we're married to a Yup'ik. Anyway, I'm still just a substitute.

All my paperwork hasn't been completed. I'm not even certified in Alaska yet.

"Why don't they want you to teach them?"

"They just don't trust me and I'm not sure that I can blame them. They're all nice to each other and soft-spoken. They think white people are craxy and steal and they're kind of right or at least compared to the way they are here. They're all harmonious and one with everything kind of stuff. Like today I went to a birthday and the whole village was invited. They fed everybody including me. I feel like an intruder here and I'm not sure that I can do them any good seeing as I can't even take care of myself. I'm the one doing all the learning which is fine for me but the whole picture doesn't fit."

"Sounds interesting."

"I'll give it some more time but I'm a little worried about winter. At least now I can get water that drains off the roof but the men are supposed to chop the ice to melt water in the winter. I don't have a man."

"You might have a tough time there."

"I don't know. It might be all right. At least they like me. The other white teachers haven't been going to steams and Harold went in and scolded Donna in the middle of her class for disciplining her son. Just regular classroom management. I was surprised but maybe she deserved it. Who can say if you weren't there, right?"

"It'll be okay." One way or another I think as I regretfully say goodbye. Gazing out the window I feel like I can see his face spread across the sky in the clouds. They look so pretty tonight ~ a pink and orange haze stretched out in the cirrus clouds over the bay. Maybe we can meet in the clouds. The distance weighs on me. The plywood house feels like a cold prison cell.

Anastasia greets me in the lounge this morning where I'm making copies for the math lesson.

"Did you get sick?"

"No," I say wondering what she's talking about.

"We all felt sick this morning from the fish," she says laughing lightly. "We were worried maybe you got sick too."

"No, I feel fine. It was a wonderful meal. Thank you so much."

Monday morning is actually treating me well. My watermelon jellybeans give me some variety in my breakfast of Ritz and peanut butter. I'm out of jelly. Sophie walks by in a long, dull colored skirt like Anastasia is wearing.

"Good morning," she says.

"Good morning," I say with some jellybeans in my mouth.

"Don't talk with your mouth full. That's a Gusuk rule not a Yup'ik rule," she chides with a big grin. I feel like I'm given the chance to look at the Sun without harm to my eyes whenever she smiles at me.

Please let me see the students smile today. Please, please let this day go okay. Ingrid is taking a vacation this week so I feel a little more scared.

The morning starts out smoothly with the multiplication review until I try to introduce fractions.

"Cheeeap," Aaron says from his seat. Trenton joins in. "Cheeap…what is this anyway?" I see Ruvim looking proud and suspicious staring at me as if I'm trying to teach them how to make a bomb to blow up the village.

"Fractions are good. They can help you share things evenly with your friends." How can I make this seem important to a communal group of people?

"Who wants to volunteer to come up to the board?" They all look at me suspiciously, except Helen with her big black eyes full out glaring at me. A tall, skinny, pale man with a light brown mustache walks into the room and sits down in the back. The class doesn't even look at him making me think they know who he is. Ruvim's face tightens and he sits up even straighter in his seat. Even with his full cheeks and little pursed mouth his eyes emanate the intent of a warrior. His buzz cut and broad shoulders make him look ready for battle. I'm guessing it's against the man who just walked in without warning of introduction.

I pause giving the man a forced smile and a chance to introduce himself but he motions for me to continue. It's an irksome, piddly wave of his hand that would appear as though he's trying not to be disruptive but he knows he is and is enjoying the discomfort he brings to the room.

Problem is that when I teach it's as if I am talking to a close friend about something important and private and when someone walks in to watch I feel like I have to change topic altogether. Any progress that could have been make because we were in an open, honest and vulnerable position is stolen because our safe bubble is broken.

"Ruth, Jessica, will you come up please?" They squirm and smile but make their way up beside me. Whenever they finish an assignment they draw me pictures of pretty ladies with hearts and diamonds around them to hang around my desk. Nina had been drawing me lots of pictures as well of women with hearts around their Egyptian eyes and high arched brows. I wait seeing if anyone is getting brave but no one else walks up.

"Nina, will you come up too please?" She hops up.

"Okay, how about three boys?" Robert walks up smiling shyly.

"Aaron, do you want to come up?" I see a little interest start to glimmer in his eyes. So far he has liked having the attention on him. He walks up with a rebellious smirk on his face. Mark follows Aaron so now I have six of the fifteen students lined up next to the blackboard.

"Now if I ask half of you to sit down, does anyone know how many that will be?" I ask trying to start the lesson with a familiar term. I'm still in the process of assessing their prior knowledge so this will be an experiment. The thing I'm most concerned with is making progress. Ruth looks at the line easily counting since she is a head taller than everyone else.

"Three," she says confidently. A few of the students look worried.

"That's right. Good job. If there are six of you and you split up into two equal groups yo would have three in each group to make two equal groups," I say using my arm to cut the line in half.

"Now I'd like each of you girls to pick someone. Nina picks Helen who crosses her arms across her chest and sticks out her lower lip. So she picks Joseph instead. Oh great. So far Joseph has had half of the class in hysterics on more than one occasion…myself included. His face is flexible like Jim Carry's and his teeth are very crooked, big and bucked out which adds to the faces he's so skilled at making. He had Lenny doubled over on his large belly, while the rest of him shook. Joseph was dancing around him making ten hundred different faces with in about twenty seconds. It taught me that I could write with my left and right hand on the board so not to turn my back.

I call Carl up who is usually quiet to make it an even eight.

"How many would have to sit down now if I asked half of you to do so?" I ask giving Ruth a look to let others answer. She nods understanding my plan.

They all look at each other dubiously so rather than make them feel awkward and wait it out past ten seconds I start to explain but Aaron interrupts.

"This is cheeap. I don't want to play."

"Yeah, cheeap," half of the others join in.

"Good, half of you said cheeap. We'll get this," I say turning my head away. I watch as the class vetoes the lesson in front of some creepy man who seems to think he has the right to just walk in, sit and judge in the middle of a lesson.

"Okay, why don't you practice the next page of multiplication facts in your work book. They've enjoyed this and trusted their own work last week. I make my way to the back of the class to question the visitor.

"Can I help you?"

"Oh no, I'm the Bush psychologist. The students call me Dick. I just came in to observe and get a group going to meet for the year on Tuesdays. Do you have three you would like me to take?" he asks eyeing the room like he knows exactly who he wants. I know nothing about this and have no idea who I want to go with this person who gives me the creeps. No one really.

"Do I have to tell you right now?"

"No, I'll be back tomorrow but if I could speak with Aaron…Miss Strauss? Is that right? It seems he's having some difficulty. Aaron throws another paper airplane.

"Sure." Dick corners Aaron as he races over to the big window and sits himself on the heater in a sulking position. Great. Another helper to mess things up. Thank goodness it's almost time for Sophie to come in and tach Yup'ik so I can critique their rough draft writing samples for the day.

At lunch time Patricia greets me in the lounge with some of their leftover stew. She even warms it up for me in the microwave before she gives it to me. I enjoy the meal in the comfort of her reminding me of the comfort and protection my own mom has given me. Now I understand the meaning of bittersweet.

My mom used to limit the number of sleepovers I went to because I'd always be cranky for the next week from staying up too late. She'd let me sit on her warm sunned lap at the beach after I'd been in the ater till I was shivering. She'd make me banana mild shakes when I got my braces tightened and my mouth hurt. Please, Mom, let your package come today.

I race to the post office. My feet swim in my clunky boots to check my PO box. I pop two jellybeans for good luck. They key fits into box 244 neatly and I peer inside. First I think there is nothing and then I see a thin, white slip lying face down. Quickly I pull it out as a mother and child watch me curiously. I have a package! I hand the slip over to the postmaster with all the reserve I can muster.

She takes her time milling around looking through boxes until finally she finds mine and slowly hands it over.

"Quayana," I say in my best guttural accent. Patricia and Leslie have been giving me lessons. Thank you is one of the easier words. So far, the business people don't appear to appreciate my attempts to speak their language. She turns away. Her tight bun says good riddance.

It's okay though because Daniel's package has made it to me so at least I know she's not sabotaging my mail. In uncharacteristic style of the Yup'iks I run home across the boardwalk clumping loudly past the houses. A few kids come outside to watch me run by in my dress and boots. A little rain is falling so I clutch the worn cardboard box shaped like a pillow under my coat. I tromp up the stairs and fumble with the key to my pad lock. Inside the house I pull the light switch to the 40 watt bulb screwed into the ceiling to shed a little light on the treasure before me:

Emily Strauss

PO Box 244

Edinak, Alaska 99611

I collapse into the couch and read the letter over and over smiling from ear to ear. The chill of the tundra is blown away. Warmth takes over.

I tear into the package. It's like a Mary Poppin's carpet bag with items that keep appearing. Compact Discs to go with the player my mom is sending. Mozart, Sara Mclachlan along with some others we'd listened to. Then snickers bars – king size! I rip the plastic off and bite off a big piece swallowing it like a dog before it's fully chewed. All my taching files are enclosed. My beloved 'magic carpet.' I found the antique rug with frayed tassels when I was fourteen. It's mostly a deep red but the other colors and designs remind me of a forest filled with the faces of wolves and wild flowers with a white sun in the center.

Pasta is under the rug with the stainer I'd asked for. Thank you. Quayana. I can make my own dinner tonight! Lastly I find a zip lock bag with a big, magenta, zinnia inside. It still has a scent. Carefully I place it in my Bible.

I pull out the pots Sophie lent to me and dip one into the water bucket on the floor to start it boiling on the burner. The dinner is cooked with ease and I have my own dinner in my empty, little house. I stare at the blank, bright, yellow wall and listen to the wind blowing around the house making it sway a little on its stilts. My spaghetti gets cold before I finish. The fork drops limply to the plate still in my hand. What am I doing here?

My shy beeping alarm wakes me in the morning. My body feels like a board on the boards that I rest. My stomach growls as I run my hand over the growing valley between my hips. Please let this day go okay. I spin on my butt dropping my feet on the magic carpet. That lifts my spirits a little. The blue comforter pulls up evenly making it look like a huge pillow that I would like to dive back into. I could disappear into a deep, warm ocan. But if I tried that I would crash down on the hard wood directly beneath the thin layer of down feathers. Maybe my mom's package will arrive today.

This is the second day without Ingrid, which I fear will be trouble. I brush my teeth in the school bathroom which has running water and look myself in the mirror thinking I can give myself a pep talk but I look all washed out. The only color difference is the deep blue circles under my eyes. At least my hair is clean from the steams each night. Not having a mirror at home prevents me from seeing the kind of French braid I've been doing. The shark fins my brother used to give me pulling out just a little hair on top are back. I push the hair that's sticking out under some other hair that is pulled back smoothly. At least with my hair back it takes away one of my differences from the Yup'iks.

"Why are there different colors in your eyes?" Joseph the comedian asks me seriously. Lining up for meals seems to be their favorite time to inspect and comment on my appearance.

"I don't know Joseph. That's just the way I am." The line is horsing around a little so with the help of Nina's mom I learned to say 'Be good.'

"Why don't you have a Yup'ik sign?" she asked. I looked up to the rules above the board along with the stop sign program the psychologists told us to put up and wondered what she meant.

"The rooms have Yup'ik and English signs," she says with concern but trying to be helpful, which was more information than anyone else had given me. They all told me to feel free and ask questions but I didn't know enough to ask any questions.

"They like you," she says looking at the pictures they've made hanging behind my desk. Even Aaron drew a picture of a mobster for me. I join her gaze at the colorful hearts, balloons, rainbows and pretty faces. They may like me but they don't trust me. I smile to her happy to have someone coming right out giving me their opinions. She looks at me for a moment sympathetically and then darts out the door. Therefore, I'll have to make a Yup'ik sign and an English sign to hang on the board to turn back and forth to signify how the students hould speak. I try out the Yup'ik she taught me. "Asickchaluten! (spelled phontetically for 'be good'. I say trying to imitate Ingrid's stern voice. The students laugh at my accent but they do improve their line a little. I turn and smile trying not to show it as we head down to breakfast.

While they eat I put up the Yup'ik alphabet and the Yup'ik/Ennglish sign. The alphabet goes above the long window in the class. The big, clean, east facing window view is still the flat tundra shrouded in heavy mist and low clouds. The tundra looks brighter than when I walked to school making me think the Sun rises at about 9:00 AM now. It seems to be rising later and setting earlier at a great rate in the last week. I wonder how long it will take for the times of the Sun's rising and setting to meet at Edinak's parallel at just above 60 degrees. I've never been up this high on the Earth before. My boss in Glacier told me it wouldn't be pitch black all the time more like dusk in the middle of the day.

"You'll see," say the Yup'ik's. Sophie told me she likes the summer better.

I finish putting up the 18 letters of the Yup'ik alphabet before I get them from breakfast but it takes me a few times spacing the letters evenly above the window. They have most of the same letters as the English alphabet. They also have a few joined letters to make one sound. Ruth the brave one is the only one to do her job this morning. The date is on the board.

Tuesday, September 9, 1997. Only three of the fifteen students signed in this morning but they're all here.

"You're writing assignment today is: 'What I like about Winter.' Robert passes out the paper. His think eyebrows and lashes barely hide his serious look about his task. He makes sure he hands just one piece of paper out to each student. His plaid ironed shirt makes him look like a teacher amongst the T-shirts his classmates wear. A feeling like when Sophie is in the room falls nicely over the class as they set to work writing about winter. I set to work deciding which pen-pal letter should go to which student. I think it will be best to place boys with boys and girls with girls and then see who wants another letter since Ann's class has more students.

A paper airplane flies across the room signifying that Aaron is finished.

"Did you proof read it?" I ask

"You're gonna leave here, aren't you?" Aaron demands.

"Did you proofread?"

"I want you to leave here."

I think it would be best to turn my cheek in this discussion like the Yup'iks do. Maybe he misses his mom being in the classroom. I turn to help some other students proof read curious to see what winter will be like and anxious to escape Aaron.

"Stalin! You're a poet!" I say delighted after reading his paper.

"What's a poet?" Stalin asks in his voice deeper than any man's I've heard.

"It's someone who writes well and makes the words join together nicely," I say not wanting to get into too deep a discussion since Sophie will be in soon. Gives me an idea to do a poetry unit.

Sophie comes in just in time. It seems as soon as I start teaching them someone gets ornery. They're taking turns distracting my attention from teaching so I won't influence them. This time it's Trenton with the fawn eyes.

"Cheeeapp, poet." Stalin is saved from his curiosity and my brainwashing. Stalin shakes his head a little and looks strangely at what he wrote. "The winter snow falls on the village. The white, white snow. I run on the snow. The arctic fox chases me."

As I continue to read the rest of the class's first drafts Ifind that they play a lot on their snow cats chased by the arctic foxes, dig tunnels, snow caves and hide from the wind, the cold and the dark. The conditions almost sound appealing. Perfect for hibernating.

From my desk I hear and see the sounds of Sophie's lesson flowing along with attentive, sweet children before her. The clouds break a little and some morning sun seeps into the room. Sophie's Yup'ik voice is gentle. She shows them pictures of grasslands with Yup'ik works below them along with black berries, fish and Yup'ik children. The students repeat the words after Sophie and I try too…a little. The students carefully write the words down practicing their spelling. Even Lenny who won't do a lick of work unless I'm doing it with him is now behaving conscientiously. Sophie's time is sadly up so we prepare for recess. I like the sunlight lighting up the room taking away the strength and glare of the fluorescent lights above us. The students face me with their backs towards the window in their ready line.

As we walk making our way down the halls I try to silence them past the doorways of the second, sixth and fourth grade classrooms. Beatrice, the second grade white teacher who is married to a Yup'ik is the only class that seems to be engaged in a productive way. The sixth grade class looks comfortably numb sitting in their seats not doing anything except watching their teacher write out spelling words. Donna's thick blond braid whips around as she frantically passes out Mammoth tokens for good behavior as Cory calls out, "Cheap!"

My class walks out into the bright sunny day. I close my eyes ad soak in the vitamin D. The students turn their heads from the Sun like holy men from a pin up girl. "Cheeeap! It's too bright!" Aaron groans.

"Cheeap maann," Mark says holding his forearm up in front of his eyes. They all join in blocking out, turning away and growling at the Sun. The girls sans Helen huddle together protecting each other. I chuckle at Daniel's point about different perspectives. I cut recess short and continue the reading assessment for groups.

Ruvim is next. Tall, sweet and proud, he walks slowly over to the reading table while the rests of the class reads silently.

"How about if I read a page and then you read a page?" I ask almost surprised he's willing to try. He gives me a very small, slow nod with his little mouth pursed weighing the safety of my proposal. After all I might be a crazy, white woman who steals. He reads slowly checking my expressions every other word so I nod each time he looks at me trying to look calm.

"The boy is sss…ss…ssrr."

"That's good, take it in parts," I say covering all but the first syllable of the word and then the next helping him sound it out and then put it together.

"Sur…priz…ed," he says slowly and then with more confidence.

"That's it!" I say letting out some white girl enthusiasm. Ruvim almost smiles but then recoils a little falling back into his proud stare. Not wanting to push things I dismiss him and call on Helen but she won't even come over to the reading table. Instead, she crosses her arms, sticks out her lower lip and drops her chin onto her chest.

Robert's dad comes into the class after school smiling warmly at another day gone by.

"How are you doing?"

"I don't know. I don't think I have an understanding about things here to tach these kids on their terms." A little progress was made in terms of tolerance of my presence rather than acceptance as their teacher.

"Oh you're doing fine. You just need to give them a little more time." He says encouragingly. But thinking to myself the only white teachers accepted here as teachers are the ones married to Yup'iks. I just wanted a teaching job and some Alaska adventuring.

"Robert is wonderful. I don't know what I'd do without him in here." I say which is true. I think he is the only one willing to actually let me be his teacher. So far he is the only one to heed my corrections on his rough drafts and make those corrections on his second drafts for writing. Maybe because their family has moved around he's more accepting of different people. But why should the others? All they see of Gusuk's is on television where we do seem crazy or like overbearing invaders like the Gusuk barges floating in flooding their canals. Gusuk boats look like rhinos sitting with birds on a wire compared to the self sufficient fishing boats of the Yup'iks. Granted they like their plywood houses and all terrain vehicles but that's no skin off a Gusuk's backs to trade. Invade and attack a people's culture with Gusuk teachers like myself – that's a lot of skin off the Yup'iks backs. Such a sideways belittlement. What a lousy way to dominate. Domination at all. Makes me feel like a termite.

Edinak is a village that's stayed close to its values. They don't drink alcohol for one thing. I don't want to be a life force to deflect in any community. Especially one that lives as harmoniously with the other people as it does with the land.

Edinak lives in cooperation. That takes intelligence, control, and respect of which I'm not confident I could learn after 24 years of capitalistic rearing. I'd be willing to leave them alone and mind my own business though. Or at least ask them what they want and don't want and how they want to trade.

Harold tells me smiling that he wants to five Patricia running water but she doesn't want it.

"I'll lose my muscles," she says carrying a bucket in each of her strong hands.

Chapter

I practically take off running after school to see if my mom's care package came in. I reflect without changing my behavior that the school's new teacher must look rather undignified running in skirts and huge rubber boots to the post office every day.

They Yup'iks that I've seen are always strolling peacefully from place to place. I think there is a quoted about civilized people never hurrying.

Approaching the post office puts a submissive spell over me and I slow my gallop to a gate and then to a forced stroll as I walk in and check my box. Nothing. This has to be wrong.

"Did I get a package today?" I ask meekly trying not to sound desperate.

"No the plane hasn't come in yet today and it probably won't in time," she says surprising me with so much information but maybe because it's bad news. Or maybe she feels a little pity for my sallow appearance.

I walk back over the bridge with a new attitude towards the tundra. I wish I'm a piece of the grass waving in the wind. The blades of greens and yellows all look healthy and iridescent in the little bit of Sun that makes its way through the low clouds. The long grass next to the canals looks pretty in its riparian zone like it knows it's well adapted to its place. Confident grass. Confidence.

Wiping my heavy, clunky boots off the best I can I trudge back into the school to do some correcting when Aaron's dad confronts me all irritated from behind.

"Look at the floor. I just vacuumed and look behind you." There is a line of mud leading back to the door that I just came in right to my heels.

"I'm sorry. I'll clean it up," I say soothing his scolding into surprise. I start to clean it up but then he finishes with expertise. He takes me outside to the grates and demonstrates how to wipe off the huge amounts of mud that collect on my feet in just a short walk. I decide to always change into my school shoes at the door from then on instead of in the classroom.

I shake off the scolding on my way back to the classroom when Sophie's tall, graceful stature greet me in the hall. Her eyes carry a look of more concern that usual.

"Emmy, do you know about the comet?" she asks slowly possibly questioning if she should ask me.

"Yes, I saw it last winter from West Glacier." I got up at five in the morning surrounded by five feet of snow to watch Hail Bop streaming through the star filled sky. All these sparkling diamonds neatly arranged in the black night except for one traveling quickly on its own course. Sophie pauses her concerned expression growing.

"Will it end the world?" she asks.

"I don't think so. They're balls of ice and dust moving through space and the Sun evaporates the ice to make the tail we see. I don't think we need to worry about it," I say hoping what I'm saying is true. Although the layers of Earth suggest comets made the dinosaurs extinct. That didn't exactly end the world. Some mammals, birds and other species survived. The energy of life just took on new forms.

I contemplate continuing the discussion but decide that might not be appropriate yet. Sophie nods slowly taking in and weighing the validity of what I say. Think she buys a little of it which makes me feel a connection. Next if only my mom's care package came in.

Always a trade off. The lack of food, rather my pickiness and cheapness inspires an idea for a science unit on adaptations instead of the book's units that don't really relate to the lives of these students. The unit can be around bird adaptations since there are a lot of ducks around the village as well as some owls. Slowly I head home until I'm greeted by Ruth, Jessica and Sandy.

"What are you doing?" Ruth asks thoughtfully.

"Going home I guess."

"Can we come with you?" Jessica asks sweetly.

"Sure," I say the three girls lifting my spirits. We walk circling each other across the boardwalk past the nice teacheridges that are like modern day condos, running water and all. That's where the Yup'ik English teacher lives with her Gusuk husband who also taches a high school subject. I'm surprised by the bitter feeling I have towards the whites that are married to Yup'iks.

The girls rotate walking in front of me taking turns to talk. They cheer my mood but I keep looking to the sky for the plane carrying my food.

"Why do you keep looking at the sky?" Ruth asks always observant. She starts to look too. Her shoulders are almost level with mine.

"My mom sent me some food and I thought it would arrive today." All eyes turn to the tarp of clouds.

"We'll probably hear it before we see it." I say hopeful from my companion's interest. I pass out a watermelon jellybean to each of the three girls from my dwindling supply to try and prove to myself that I have faith that more food is on the way but they don't like its sweetness. Our collective choice to stop at the juncture of the post office and my house on the boardwalk makes me more hopeful. We all wait looking at the sky trying to figure out exactly what direction the plane will come from.

"I think that way," Jessica says pointing in the direction of the place she was looking when she'd asked me if there are trees where I'm from.

"No, probably more to the right." Ruth says with confidence. Sandy shrugs her shoulders gently scanning the whole sky east of the village. At least we all agree on that. I look at my watch. The post office will be closed in another twenty minutes. Hurry food, hurry.

"I think I hear something," Sandy says softly putting her hand to her ear the way Daniel did on our hike out from Kinnerly Mountain in the near pitch-black night.

I think it was a new moon. Daniel and I were pretty much lost in the thickest part of the woods trying to make our way to Kintla Lake and creek. Daniel kept stopping whenever I tripped over a log to hear where the sound of water was coming from. At first, I thought he was being silly cupping his hand around his ear but sure enough when I tried it the sound of the wind through the trees was amplified but I couldn't hear any water even when Daniel claimed he could. Either he got lucky or he wasn't bluffing. He led us to Kintla Lake and then to the creek where we crossed in the dark.

The icy water up to our waist pushed hard against us. We waked across arms around each other for support. Then by feeling with his feet back in the woods, he found the trail to our campsite and stayed on the trail dented wide enough for one foot at a time.

"If bears can follow the trails in the dark, I figure I can too," he instructed. I tried to focus on the back of Daniel's white shirt to guide me. I walked as fast as I could. Near delirium from fatigue and hunger I stumbled against the edge of the trail padded down by hikers and animals. The blur of his white shirt like a ghost leading through the darkest corridor of time.

The peanut butter we ate when we got back to the tent stung the roof of my mouth from the electrolytes being so far depleted. But I couldn't have been happier lying down in the tent next to him after our first big hike together climbing Kinnerly. I held on to him as we fell asleep amazed that I hadn't felt scared hiking through grizzly country in the dark. I kind of felt he was one of them.

"Yes, I do hear a plane!" Sandy says cupping her hand more tightly around her ear. Quickly we all look at the sky trying to be the first to see where the sound is coming from but we're all wrong. We don't see the plane until it's on its final turn towards the runway.

"There it is!" Jessica shouts turning us all in the other direction. The short, dirt runway is the only solid surface in the village. It welcomes the plane into our sights.

The 'handsome man' from the airport in Bethel loads the boxes in the cart behind his hour-wheeler smiling at us as if to say you'll have to wait. Three minutes until the post office closes.

We chase the ATV down the boardwalk to the post office where the postmaster is waiting with the back garage door open for delivery.

"Are any of those for Emily Strauss?" I must look pathetic because she looks at me half smiling.

"Wait," she says emphasizing the 't'. She sorts through everything with no response. My shoulders sag along with the three girls as we turn to leave.

"Wait," she says again holding a box out to me. Grabbing the box the girls and I rush back to my house where I rip open the package to see what feast is inside. My feverish behavior has the three girls standing very still.

"Cookies!" Orange juice! Rolos! Beans! Cheese and crackers, soup… milk! She sent me mild!" I hand the girls the cookie package and rip out the ice-pack and mild from its plastic bag guzzling out of the container until I remember myself and stop. I should ration it. I dig through more food: slim jims, tuna, twinkies…twinkies? I like Twinkies. My mom is a nut she's also a life savor. I slow down enough to read her note.

"September 4, 1997

Had a hard time buying these things. Was not sure what you wanted. Make a LIST for me. Some things that are hard to get there.

I know when we went to New Zealand we had trouble figuring out what to eat. We finally learned to eat what the Kiwis do.

Sending this on Thursday the 4th. Let me know when you get it. Remember it always takes you 2 weeks to adjust.

Lots of love, Mom'

It took four days for it to reach me and everything is hard to by here except Crisco and onions. Thank you, Mom! Thank you, thank you, thank you. The girls and I have a little feast in the kitchen. It feels like Thanksgiving. I'm glad they turn their noses up to most of the food my mom sent. I give them some of the dried fish Patricia had given me.

5:30 PM and good coma is setting in. It's so relaxing to be full. The Sun is starting to set through the little window in the living room where I hung the prism. Sandy notices the first few rainbows on the yellow wall opposite the window.

"How did that get there?" she asks startled by the little rainbows on the wall. I continue to chew on the dried fruit my mom sent.

"How do you think it got there?" I ask hoping to engage a lesson without them noticing and deflecting it like they might in the classroom. They all look around the nearly empty living room until Ruth catches the prism twinkling in the window.

"There!" she says triumphantly. "That's doing it!"

"Yes, but how?" I ask egging her on while switching over to the Twinkies. All three pause contemplating the matter.

"It's just like a rainbow with the Sun and rain. How does the rain drop of the prism make all those colors out of the Sun?"

"Do you know how?" Ruth asks me.

"Yes," I say smirking. Hiding in the kitchen I collect my crayons and draw a picture of the Sun, its light in all the colors of the rainbow in their bending order and then cover it with a flap of white paper with the white light on it.

"Do you think the light from the Sun has anything inside it? Like adutaq is not just akutaq but there are parts to it to make up the ice cream that we don't see like the sugar and water but they are in there, right?" I ask hoping that there is only one recipe in the village for akutaq and that's the one I used.

"Yes, they say slowly and suspiciously.

"Well pull off the flap of sunlight to find what's inside it." I tell them smiling. Jessica smiles back, her big smile and lifts the flap.

"So all those colors are in the Sun light?" Ruth asks dubiously.

"Uhh, huhh," I say wondering how I'll explain the next part seeing the confused expressions on their faces.

"So the rain or the prism or crystal act like a strainer for soup or stew. When you look in the pot all you might see is the dark broth but if you poured it through a strainer, chunks of onion or meat would come out, right?" They shake their heads yes, looking like they mean it.

"That's what the rain and the prism do. They separate and show us all the colors hiding in the Sun's light."

"And the rainbow shows us God's promise," Ruth says adding to the lesson.

Watching the three girls gently twirl the prism to study the movements of the dancing rainbows on the wall stills me. I put the Twinkie down to watch the wonder of learning. Joy and peace tap my shoulder having taught here in Edinak.

My reverie is broken by a surge from all the sugar.

"Do you want to go for a run?" I ask them still inspecting the prism hanging from the window by a pale blue string of wool yarn. They all look at each other.

"Sure, we could run towards the dump. Have you been there yet?" Ruth asks as the spokes person.

"No but that sounds good. How far is it?"

"It's a ways out of the village."

We all head out the main door then the arctic entrance door and down the steps past the steam hut, over the bridge and we're pretty much out of the village running on the soft wood planks of the boardwalk. It's the lone section of the boardwalk like a tail off a tadpole. It leads us out to the Bering Sea. The village looks smaller and smaller in a hurry as we head west towards the dump.

Just about when I can see a tall, wire fence off in the distance the girls start to lag behind. When the wind blows in our direction, a faint smell of sewage enters my Gusuk nose reminding me of the days when my front yard growing up had a leaky septic tank.

"Don't stop, we're almost there," I say watching them slowing to a walk. I run back feeling free, full and getting a cramp. No luck. They drag their feet as I try to spur them on. Ruth joins me for a little while longer but I outrun her too reaching the end of the boardwalk ad the start of the waste sight. I understand why they slowed down.

The smell of human waste is strong. Next to the Olympic size pool of human waste is an equally sized pile of old furniture, wrappers, clothes and other garbage.

Plugging my nose, I wait for the girls who seem to be slowing even more. Jessica has stopped on the swaying bridge section. Strange because the bridge looked like it was stiff on the tundra.

The tundra still looks mostly flat with a few slopes and who would know where it was solid enough to walk on and where you would sink in and be swallowed by the innocent looking grass. Maybe that's how the Yup'iks feel about me. That's why they're so careful not to listen to me too long. They might sink into the world of a Gusuk.

How hard that would be to fear your teacher's intentions. They are so gracious to keep me company or am I an amusement like a one-woman circus show? If they are patient with me maybe they can turn the invader into one of their own.

I rest at the dump to scan the horizon. Far towards the Bering Sea are six brown structures that look like igloo shaped houses. I run back to the girls to ask them what they are.

"That's the old village. The houses used to be made of mud," Ruth instructs. Sandy and Jessica nod curiously looking out towards the village of their ancestors. The mud houses blend so well with the browns and tans in the fall grasses. I wonder how it was to live with no heat in the winter out there. The half a dozen little, mud houses look peaceful resting far away on the tundra by the sea.

Wednesday morning and my magic carpet only comforts my feet. Everything else aches. My back from the floor and my brain from fear of the day. I feel like an impossible victory is before me. Partly because it's one that I shouldn't be fighting or win. To be a trusted teacher in a place where I can't take care of myself. Thankfully I have cereal and orange juice for breakfast. I can feel the vitamin C absorbing into my blook in record time. My throat opens for the milk like an alcoholic for whiskey.

Now I can face the day with at least the security that I'm not at risk of scurvy. School provides running water so I pack my toothbrush and toothpaste up and head out on the boardwalk amongst the pale plywood houses just becoming visible in the dawn before the rising Sun. I can see enough tht it looks like another cloudy day.

Today at recess rather than chase the kids around keeping them off the dilapidated fence I try to start a game that's refused by all. Instead they teach me their village game. One half of the class stands against the playground court. The tam decides what village they're from and what activity they will pantomime for the side against the fence to figure out. When they do they yell out the activity. If it's the right activity the team acting it out runs back to their side without being tagged. Who ever isn't tagged stays in the game until no one is left.

The first team to be up has their backs to the still unused special education building. Huddling up, they decide what to pantomime while the other side watches trying to hear or see any clues. The performers make their way to the middle of the court.

"Where are you from?" asks the guessing side.

"Chefornak."

"What do you do?" Immediatley the performing side starts pantomiming…something.

"Fishing! Hunting?!" The performers keep acting letting the guessing side know they're not correct yet.

From the looks of them I'm not sure they're all doing the same thing. Elbows and knees are going in all directions. It looks cute but…even chubby Lenny is moving all around. All of them are smiling and laughing.

"Drumming!" Ruth shouts and the performers run back to their side chased by their opponents. Mark, Jessica and Stalin catch Nina, Helen and Lenny.

Finally a successful recess. Maybe I should let the kids teach the rest of the day too.

I learned a lot of the other villages names and what activities each village specializes in. I'm anxious to tell Daniel he's right about the drums.

We make our way back into the classroom more calmly than usual so I don't ask any questions. I feel hopeful about the science lesson and a little guilty for teaching animal adaptations when Ingrid told me not to teach science.

"Clear your desks please. Put your paper airplanes away." I say eyeing Aaron who is actually more responsive today. Makes me wonder what his mom's presence does to my accountability. I don't know what she's saying to them in Yup'ik.

Sticking some pictures of birds to the board on one side and bird food on the other a little feeling of curiosity grows in the room as voices subside. Even Ruvim's face is expressing some interest breaking from his usual proud, defensive look. His eyebrows aren't as stitched together and his mouth is not as pursed. Helen remains dubious, scowling at me with her head tilted down. If looks could kill Helen would have me dead by now.

I write Animal Adaptations on the board above the pictures of the birds.

"We're going to learn what adaptations are through different kinds of birds. Any ideas what an adaptation is?" They all study the picture of the owl. The dick. And the songbird. The owl and the dick had made an appearance already in the village so I knew at least these two would be part of a pertinent lesson. Unfortunately, I'm not getting any responses or guesses. Only looks of concern. I give them a few moments to think.

"Okay, as we go along with the lesson try to think of some definitions for adaptation.

"Who would like to match up the bird with its food on the board?" Some time passes and Robert raises his manicured hand quite different than most fifth grade boys you'd see anywhere in the world. Carefully he puts the owl with the mouse, the duck with the fish and the songbird with the berry. He turns for approval.

"Good work!" Thank you for volunteering. Who would like to tell me why he matched when the way he did?"

"Because that's what they eat," Mark says incredulously but I see his point. He reminds me of a picture of my brother when he cut his bangs too short and at an angle. Mark has the same haircut.

"And why do they eat what they eat? Look at their beaks. What is different about the owls beak than the song birds beak?" They look at the exaggerated hooked beak of the owl and the straight beak of the songbird.

"One is straight and one is curved," Ruth says brightly getting the hang of the Socratic method.

"Yes! And what would the different beaks be good for? Why would a hooked, sharp beak be good for eating a mouse?" Is it like a knife to cut meat?" Half of the class starts to shake their heads.

"And why would the songbirds beak be good for eating berries?"

"Because it can pick up the berries," Nina says delightedly.

"Yes so if we look up the word adaptation in the dictionary what does it say?" A few of the students rush over to the dictionaries to look up the word. Ruth is the first to find it.

"Something that is changed or changes to become suitable to a new situation. 3. A hereditary alteration in an organism that facilitates its survival and reproduction." Ruth says stopping to look up to me. The rest of the class shares the confuse expression on her face. As I was taught to put definitions into my own words I ask the class to do the same. I get blank expressions.

"Let's think about ourselves. What do we have that helps us live?" I ask instantly regretting my inclusion of ourselves with the lesson concerning animals. Ruvim's expression goes back on the defense pursing his lips and furrowing his eyebrows. Sometimes I think more highly of wild animals than civilized humans but I watch their faces scowl at me. Another value difference. I should have listened to Ingrid.

"Never mind us." I say trying to emphasize that I group myself with them, which probably insults them more.

"Let's go back to the birds. Do you think the owl would be able to live without its beak?"

"No," Ruth says, one of the two remaining open to the lesson. The expression of the other thirteen students turn against me like drawn guns.

"Right. So it's beak helps it to live and tells it what to eat. So an adaptation is something that helps us live. Does that make sense? I ask getting a few more responsive looks but no answers. To assess I ask what are some adaptations of their favorite animals.

"Aaron what does a fox have that helps it live? What are its adaptations?"

"Cheap," he says, his low voice sounding like an almost cute growl.

"Okay, you can think about it. Carl what are some adaptations of the moose?" He pauses characteristically quiet.

"Anything it has that helps it live."

"It's…" he pauses looking back and forth from Trenton to Joseph and their warning stares. Carl closes his mouth and looks at his desk.

"Jessica, how about a horse?" She smiles sweetly but doesn't try.

"I like the bear. It has teeth to eat meat and plants like me." The bear. "It has long claws to dig up roots and a brain to remember where he found food." My bear. "Bears have lots of adaptations to help it live to get food, protect food and bake babies." I miss you Bear. "That's what our adaptations do. They help us live and reproduce." I look to all their eyes beseeching them to trust what I say but they sit recoiling from my words. I can almost see the shields going up around them.

An adaptation to protect them from their crazy, white teacher. Even Lenny's adoring look has turned to scorn for polluting their air with talk about science.

"Cheeap," Aaron says getting up from his seat to raid the supply closet with help from the other boys. I go over to stand in front of th door wishing I'd remembered to bring the lock for it.

"Please sit down," I say to the three boys heading towards me like war tanks.

"We're going to make a bulletin board with our hand prints. Their revolt works and we change subjects. I don't want them to tar apart the supply closet again.

I wish I'd respected their value against science even if I don't understand it.

Chapter

The Wednesday after school meeting seems to go as well as my day. All except for the hand print bulletin board, which was a success. T.J., the principal, asks if there are any problems and nobody says anything.

"That's great. I haven't had any complaints yet so that's good," he says in his friendly, deep southern accent.

"I do want to get into your classrooms soon so let me know if anytime would be better than another. What other business do we have?" He looks optimistically at the teachers sitting around the oval table under the bright fluorescent lights. Everyone is avoiding eye contact so I look out the window at the gray day.

"I would like to have a fall carnival like we did two years ago," Janet says with forced optimism. The room is silent. Her lanky husband looks down at the table. Janet breathes stiffly.

The village looks especially stark today. There's a cutting iciness in the breeze instead of just damp and cold. The pale blue of the houses overshadows the soft oranges and yellows of the grasses. The sky creeps down. The Earth is starting to freeze.

Carefully I walk on the narrow boardwalk like a tight rope walker. There is only one path to the post office. I can't cut across or skirt around.

After Aaron's father's admonishment about my boots I'm extra thorough scraping the mud on the grates before I enter the post office. Please have a letter for me. My ritual begins praying for mail. If I approach

"

the mailbox slowly, insert the key gently; peek inside the little metal door before it's fully open then there will be a letter. My heart races all the while. The white envelope in my small metal PO box looks like a slice of sunlight.

I hustle home feeling a little more resilient like I can hold up the sky long enough to get in my hose and shovel some food down. Making myself comfortable on the sagging couch I take out my antique, marble like metal letter opener that my mom and I found in Vermont. It was only a dollar and almost buried amongst some wooden boxes and glass teacups. I saw it because of its handle. A marble horse rearing on its hind legs with gold painted on his hoofs, ears and billowing tail. It feels so solid and heavy in my hands. Gently I stick the tip under the corner of the envelope so I won't tear anything Daniel has written.

I spin further into euphoria from Daniel's letter at the Ardok's steam. The heat from the water is warming me like he does. I feel drunk, hot and relaxed. Leslie knocks me out of my reverie.

"Your turn to pour," she says surprising me with the honor. I hold on to the stick attached to the soup can, fill it with hot water from the bin attached to the barrel with the fire inside that heats the rocks attached to the top of it. Carefully I try to evenly pour the water over the slate looking rocks. Although the thick haze of moisture in the little wooden room keeps me from seeing clearly even three feet away over the drop in-between our landing and the barrel. I stop pouring when the heat starts to prickle on my back like cheese under a broiler. It feels so good.

"That's enough," Leslie says sounding like Harold in his slow yet authoritative tone always with an inflection and emphasis on the last syllable. Patricia had taken a relatively quick steam. Maybe an hour so Leslie and I have the three by two foot landing to ourselves.

"How are you so skinny?" Leslie asks poking at my ribs. It's easy around here with the staples being Crisco and dried fish. I look at her round, fleshy body then back to me. I look skinny in comparison.

"I don't know. My brother and I were really skinny growing up. We're filling out now though." When we go inside we pass the puppy that's leg is getting better and Patricia points to a red square on one of her blankets.

"How do people get hair this color?" she asks shyly.

"I don't know. They're just born that way or they dyed it red."

"They buy is at the store?"

"Sometimes, but I have some friends that were born with red hair." Her silky black hair falls over her shoulder as her chin tilts forward questioning me, "out of a box."

"Eemmilyy," Harold says sitting on the floor in front of the TV leaning against the couch. "Let Patricia give you a message. She is magic. She can find where you hurt and fix it." I look at Patricia to see if she is up for it.

"Come on, let her. Sit down next to me," Harold continues. So I sit on the floor with my back against the couch.

Patricia begins feeling around my neck and upper back gently not really doing much and then with a stabbing thumb she pushes in near my shoulder blade and gives my whole body a release of tension. Harold is right. She feels around my back for another spot and presses in on it near my lower back. Once again she's connected to something that's connected to heat feels like wires passing heat all thought me and then another deep relaxation.

Harold nods to me knowingly. Nonchalantly he turns on the news to the spokesman in Anchorage talking about a twenty one year old man raping and shooting a woman.

"Young men," Harold says like it's a condition to be pitied.

Instead of finishing the news they put in the movie 'Beetle Juice' with Michael Keaton. I watch as a stark, white, ghost faced man with electrified hair and a striped suit runs around after a screaming white woman. No wonder they think white people are crazy.

"Are you going to come back after the in-service in Bethel?" Patricia asks shaking out her hands. Tomorrow night all the teachers will be flown back to the armpit of Alaska for an in-service on how to teach. I am sure the kids will be happy there is no school Friday.

"Yes. I'll come back." They ask me to spend the night but I go home.

Tonight lying on the floor I hear the wind cursing through my pillow on the thin plywood, upon the stilts five feet above the tundra.

The dawn greets me coldly. I miss Daniel and my family. I want to see their faces. Not the faces of children who don't want me for their teacher. Faces glaring at me like an evil villain. Maybe they will enjoy art.

We start the day with math which they continue to ignore me on then breakfast where the grumble at the Gusuk food. Then for writing I introduce the pen pal letters from Michigan which I hope to tie into the geography/research project on a state of their choice. Unfortunately no one wants to research Michigan. Most of them want to research Alaska.

At first the kids look like they're reading the letters quietly to themselves or at least the girls are. I used to hate when teachers lurked around behind me so I give students space but Aaron is scribbling on the letter given to him.

"What are you doing? Someone worked hard to write this letter. If you don't want it I'll take it back."

"Cheeap," he says with malice in his young, harsh voice. "Who wants this letter?" he asks rhetorically. Stalin, Mark, Trenton, Helen an Arie and Joseph join Aaron in the shredding of their Gusuk pen pal letters. My heart bleeds a little as I think of my friend working with her students to write the letters. My students rip the letters apart. Breaks my heart to say the least.

For art I try to teach them about Grandma Moses who took up her dream and love of painting when she was in her golden years - the first chance she got to have free time to enjoy her hobby. I show them her paintings and give them their own scene to color but the farm scenes wit trees and barns have nothing to do with them. Some of the students color the pater raw until it rips like the letters. Reading and grammar are the same. They do the work but they ignore any corrections and progress I try to make with them.

"He waLks the dog," Helen reads aloud.

"That was good but the L blends in with the K. It's kind of a funny way to write the word but those are the rules."

"He waLks the dog," Helen reads again with more venom in her pronunciation of the L.

At least we have gym at the end of the day. We run around the gym together and circle up to stretch. We go through a regular stretching regime which they follow until I demonstrate a split.

"Miss Strauss! You won't be able to have babies!" Joseph says in alarm. The sincere look of concern on all the kid's faces is surprising but interesting. I stand up and touch my toes to hide my giggle. The class exhales.

Getting the ball out of the closet has been a battle. Mark, Aaron and Joseph have taken to pushing their way into the supply closet, grabbing as much equipment as possible and then throwing it around the gym.

"All of you have to stand on the other side of the gym before I unlock the door to get the basketballs out." I feel like I've really wised up. Too bad I have to steal the balls to put them away.

We file outside to cool down which is something we all enjoy but getting them back in is difficult. Aaron's dad hears me outside.

"Time to come in," I say with no response from the students. I open the door for them ~ still nothing. They're all still breathing heavily from the game wiping the sweat from their foreheads and tilting their faces towards the strong wind. Except for Stalin who makes for the fourth grade class window next to the door and starts making funny faces as only he knows how. Tongue out, pulling back his lips showing his gums, rolling his eyes around laughing in his super deep, loud voice.

Aaron's dad comes out. He holds Stalin by the back of the neck leading him back to the classroom. Everyone follows them to the room.

When the class leaves I have the opportunity to go to the office where the secretary will greet me with the kids back but wasn't shy about his disapproval as he emptied the full trash cans.

"You use a lot of paper," he says crushing it down with his fist.

I punch my time card in the office.

"Oh Emily, you have a letter," Lee says quickly. "Is this what you've been waiting for?"

It says Michigan on the top. The letter I need to apply for Alaska certification and then be able to sign my contract for Edinak. For now I need to get to the runway to catch the plane for Bethel. I won't be able to steam tonight. Donna, Lilly and I are the first to arrive out by the old metal shed with graffiti on it next to the dirt runway. The weather is just like on the day I arrived ~ chilly and overcast in a way that makes me feel pressed upon. I usually like humidity but this is moisture so thick it feels like suspended rain. We all just stand there quietly. I finally find a place to sit down and rest my bags out of the mud by the shed.

"Hello Ladies," T.J. says coming up behind us. "I have your first pay checks." He hands one to each of us. I look at the envelope. It's clean and white but feels like ash sifting through and soiling my skin.

The eight-passenger plane reaches Bethel safely. All the village teachers are flown to Bethel for a Friday at the beginning of each year for training. It seems bogus to me. Donna and I are stationed at a teacher's house that is very hospitable. He offers salad, hamburger and beer. Somehow I feel funny about the alcohol since we're living in a dry village so I pass.

It's a regular house that you would see in the suburbs except for the Bethel mist hangs over. I try to listen politely to the bachelors hunting stories but there is also a mist in my brain. I can't join in the conversation. I do indulge in a hot shower though. The hot water beating down on my face feels like home.

Bedtime comes around and Donna and I are shown to a single bedroom with a double bed.

"I'll sleep on the floor. I brought my sleeping bag besides it's good for my back."

"Are you sure?" Donna asks with her big, blue, sweet eyes, wide with surprise.

"Yes. I've slept on the floor for the past three months and it's making my lower back feel better," I say reflecting on the sixteen years of back bending gymnastics I did. This seems to satisfy Donna because it should ~ it's the truth. So she gets under the bed covers.

"How…do you like this so far?" she asks shyly.

"I don't know. It's weird. I don't think they want outside teachers," I say feeling my heart start to race a little as the relaxation of the hot shower wears off.

"I know. I've already done my peace corp thing but this will help me pay off my student loans and get a job farther inland maybe in Anchorage or a smaller town like Homer."

"A friend of mine from Fairbanks wants to live in Homer. I've heard good things about it." I say.

"Where do you want to teach?" Donna asks.

"Anywhere really. No actually, someplace they want me to teach. I haven't really thought about location as much as just finding a job. I thought it would be neat to go to Alaska but not if they don't want me plus I miss Montana and Daniel.

"Who's Daniel?" she asks crossing her long, skinny legs leaning forward on the bed. I feel like saying he's my true love but I'm afraid that will sound silly.

"He's a guy I started dating at the end of this summer. He's going to South America with his family in a couple weeks but he said he might want to come visit Edinak. I don't know what he'd do there though."

"He would visit?! That would be nice. I don't think we're going to have much chance of meeting Mr. Right up here do you?"

"No but Daniel might be mine. Too bad he's so far away."

"I know I've turned down three proposals but I' not getting any younger and now I'm wondering where all the men are," Donna says partly concerned partly humored.

I don't feel humored. I recline on the floor in my sleeping bag. Adjusting my pillow I pull my hair out from under my shoulder. I feel an ache in my chest for Daniel to hold me. Instead, I get a restless night sleep.

The next morning is even less inspiring as they lead us to a seventies style building full of pasty, pale, white teachers with big circles under their eyes all sipping bad coffee and eating stale 'dog nuts' as Daniel would say. The whole place smells like bad breath. You would think with the big room and the high ceiling it would have better circulation. I'm having a hard time breathing in this large gray foyer folding a hundred or more teachers mostly twenty years older than me making me feel even more out of place.

Scanning the room I meet Sophie's eyes down by they juice. Her glum expression changes to a bright smile. I walk down to be near her. "I miss Edinak. Do you like it here?" Sophie asks.

"No, I missed steaming last night." I say watching her face soften.

From here the day is kind of a blur. They split us up into groups to go off to smaller rooms and learn about child abuse via video and how to look for signs and that we're responsible for reporting any possible cases. Al the videos show lower 48 state situations.

But here is Dick, the psychologist who interrupted my class earlier this week, talking to us like we know nothing about nothing droning on to us in a creepy, soft and patronizing voice. We're trying to tach to a community that probably doesn't know what abuse is. None of the children fear the adults, flinch at a sudden movement or express any symptoms of abuse. On the contrary all the children seem cared for by all the adults. The children come and go from hose to hose washing their hands, eating some dried fish. It's not even accepted to raise your voice to a child or to another adult. Not that they don't discipline with a squeeze on the back of the neck like I saw with Stalin but the kids respect the wishes of the adults and the adults respect the well being of the children.

There are intact families, plenty of fish and nightly steams. The stress level is low for Yup'iks. They excel at peace, faith and harmony. It's just too bad I don't like eating fish three times a day.

Maybe I can't understand why they suppress some curiosities about science but science is always changing anyway and will we ever have everything all figured out? Maybe there is a beneficial trade off. And maybe all Dick can do for these safe kids is induce his creepiness onto them.

I can hardly keep my eyes open and my head from dropping onto the desk. Sleep seems my only escape.

Finally lunchtime rolls around and I escape the room like a dog that has to pee and has been locked up for a day. Feeling opportunistic Dick catches me enjoying some broccoli and cold cuts back in the lobby.

"We all noticed you're trouble staying awake in there," he says nervously.

"I had to sleep on the floor last night." My glare is immediate. He scurries away pulling at his light brown mustache. The announcement for the next session sounds so I grab as much food as I can and find a seat.

"This video is going to show a lot of tough material so I want you to be prepared." The Gusuk speaker says seriously. The video begins quieting the audience's last murmurs.

Prejudice against blacks, against whites, against physically impaired, against mentally impaired, against financially impaired, against disease and everything else you can think of broadcasts to the audience for two painful hours.

After the depressing and unhelpful video a policeman out of the 70's stands up and asks in a southern accent, "Who is teaching in Edinak?" I along with another hew of the hundred people raise our hands.

"Ladies," he starts in his southern drawl," I don't want to alarm you," he continues in his tight uniform swinging his belly from side to side, "but we released a man from New York City jail after twelve years for sexual assaults and theft back to his home in Edinak yesterday morning. He was begging to go back to Edinak so I put the fear of God in him like you wouldn't believe," the policeman states with full confidence. "I just thought you should know because he's a big man but he swears he just want his peaceful life back."

Just before we can leave I spot a name tag with Terance Harris on it. The man who interviewed me. His posture looks like he's made of stone and his face looks like a plaster mask with gray hair that looks so neatly combed it could be a plastic helmet. His expression looks unassuming yet I feel a little hostile.

"Hello." I say trying to sound polite.

"Hello," his return is hollow but he looks at me strangely almost with some expression.

"I'm teaching in Edinak." I say getting the feeling he doesn't recognize my name tag.

"Oh, right. How is it going?" Terance asks without concern.

"It's interesting. I like the steams."

"Yes, those Yup'iks love to steam," he says forcing a small smile making it look like his face will crack if he smiles any bigger. I excuse myself feeling I have nothing to gain form this man. I was hoping he might have some insight for me but he's just making money.

Thankfully the plane leaves shortly after the in-service so I can get out of Bethel and back to Edinak's steams.

Chapter

The Ardoks are preparing the steam when I get back so I eat dinner at home and then return with my towels just in time. The men file out so now it's the women's turn. After the steam Leslie looks at me curiously but still with a little bit of a smirk.

"Can I put make-up on you?"

"Sure." I say thinking of middle school parties putting make-up on each other. She takes me back to her room. I'd never been in it before. It looks like a typical teen-age room with posters on the walls, jewelry and make-up piled on top of the dresser.

"No laughing," she says glancing at her won artwork on the walls.

"They're really good ~ a lot better than anything I could do." She motions for me to sit on her messy bed.

"I could make you a picture. Your walls are so empty."

"That would be good," I say getting comfortable on her soft bed. I love to be pampered. Leslie starts by studying her make-up and then my face.

"Do you have any Revlon stuff? That will give me a rash," I say looking at her supply of mostly Cover Girl make-up.

"No, don't worry," she says slowly with a little laugh. She starts with some base, which I don't wear, but I trust her.

"You're cheeks are so pink," she says giggling while trying to cover them with enough base to make them a soft brown. Then she works on my nose. She goes over and over with her finger on the edge of my nostrils.

"Your nose is so skinny…Mason likes to play with my nose," Leslie says finishing her study of mine. She could tell me my nose is flat out ugly. I'm so relaxed.

Next to my eyes. At least they're brown but not as dark as hers. She does them nicely in mascara and a little purple eye shadow. Carefully she glides the brush over my eyelids so softly and slowly I feel like I could fall asleep.

"Look at me," she says to examine her work. Weakly I open my eyes. "Close again," she says matter of factly putting on some more eye shadow.

"Ready for your hair?" Leslie asks.

"Sure," I say sitting up a little. She grabs the baby oil and squeezes some out into her hands rubbing them together.

"You're going to put that in my hair?!" I ask. Her giggle is deep. Don't worry, it's good for your hair," she says starting to rub it in. Okay, it feels good.

When I go to leave I look more like a Yup'ik with silky black hair from the oil and a tan face from the foundation. She also makes me a big picture of a teddy bear and a rainbow for my wall.

"You can do your make-up everyday now," she says handing me a small mirror as we walk down the gall to the living room where Harold is resting.

"Eemmilyy," Harold sings. "Do you want to go fishing with us tomorrow?"

"That would be great!"

"Come over early," he says smiling.

"Okay. Quayana."

"Ei-ii," the Ardoks all say welcome together and smile at my excitement.

Chapter

Saturday starts with the same light rain as every other morning. Today I don't fear going to school. I make some peanut butter sandwiches, fill my water bottles and pack my sleeping bag, warm clothing and rain gear (my only coat that the Ardoks don't believe is waterproof).

They're all loading blankets and cooking supplies into plastic Glad bags when I arrive. Between Harold, Patricia and her three friends we fill a dozen bags. I fear how we'll fit the five of us in the small fishing boat.

"You'll see."

We load up in the boat maybe twelve feet by six feet. I slip down the steep, muddy bank. It's the sloppiest boarding job making my mittens wet right at the start of the trip.

Harold starts up the motor in the boat, which is just a little narrower than the canal. We weave our way through the village and under two small arched bridges that take us to the bay where a bunch of fishing boats rock gently waiting to gas up. The moist, chilly air feels good on my skin waking me up.

Patricia being an aid for the fourth grade class sees a fourth grader with his family also waiting in a boat. She teases him a little calling out his name in a singsong fashion probably getting her revenge on him for the week he's given her. It works ~ he blushes trying not to look in her direction.

"Money," Harold scowls getting ready for his turn to fill his gas tanks. He pulls out a twenty like it's a dirty piece of paper. The other three ladies chuckle a little at who I know to be my saviors in Edinak.

One of the ladies is Carla, the bush pilot's wife. Carla was raised in Bethel so she doesn't laugh at me for looking young like her husband did. The oldest lady, Cheryl maybe sixty has thick-rimmed glasses like the fifties style and has a lean figure like Sophie's. The third lady, Hazel that we picked up on our way out of the village looks unhappy. All of them are dressed in very think coats. Having never gone camping on the Bering Sea I feel a little fearful that I'll be putting my three-ply coat to the test. Ruth's words ring in my head.

"It's a sin to fear. Just don't fear."

Looking out to where we're heading I can see only water until the end of the horizon. The water looks calm maybe because we're still in a sound protected from the waves of maybe it's a calm day for a long way. There is no map of compass. Only a radio that doesn't look like it works. My mother's going to kill me if I get lost out here. Harold had told me that they used to go out every weekend so I'm hoping he know what he's doing. Despite my worries I can't help but feel excited.

The morning is spent winding around in big canals that sometimes dead end so we go back out and head down the next one farther out. Down the third one we follow a group of ducks flying twice as fast as the boat. They land in the tall grass along the bank. Harold sees his opportunity, cuts the engine and glides the boat quietly towards where the ducks landed. He picks up his rifle and looks at us with his finger to his lips.

Stealthily he climbs out of the boat and up the bank on his short, strong legs. At the top he trips and falls on his face making the three ladies twitter. Patricia turns to them slightly glaring. Harold is back on his feet walking quietly away crunching through the grass nearly to his waist. Resuming his hunt he heads a little farther in, aims and shoots! Ducks go flying in every direction but he doesn't hit any. Mission denied we head back out towards the open sea which I think we finally reach because the waves increase rocking the boat and I feel lucky that I don't get sea sick. Hazel however looks unhappy and uncomfortable. She keeps her gaze focused on the stern of the boat as she sits on one of the piles of Glad bags gripping the edge of the full. Her face looks like its hanging limply from her forehead.

Mid afternoon we reach what I think is Nelson Island. It looks like the tundra in Edinak except that it has more hills making me feel the need to hike. Instead, Harold keeps me with him. After unloading the bags on the bank along with the ladies who set off with wire berry collectors and buckets to fill. They don't head off merrily like I do when I pick berries in the park. They set off with an attitude that they need to collect enough blackberries for their families for the rest of the winter.

"Do you know how to fish?" Harold asks me.

"Kind of. I used to go fishing with my Pop and I went a few times this summer but I didn't catch anything."

"I'll show you fishing." Harold says. We head out into the canal and set to work untangling the net. He takes a pole with a big bobber out and strings it through one end of the net and puts it in the water next to the bank. Then he motors over to the other side of the canal stringing the net out behind him and does the same to the other side.

"Now we leave and let the fish come to the net."

Okay I think warmed up from the weight of pulling the net around.

"Why don't you go do some woman stuff for a while," he says handing me a berry picker. I hold on to the handle inspecting the comb like prongs on the end leading to the cup at the bottom. We make it back to the supplies so I head up the hill to help the women.

The picking device is a little awkward at first but eventually I find the angle to scoop up the berries and not the whole plant, which is nestled closely to the ground. With just a little tug I can hear if it's starting to rip at the stems and roots.

My spirits lift despite the gloomy weather. I'm finally being useful to these beautiful people as I divide the berries I pick between the woman's buckets.

"Thank you!" They say seemingly surprised. I look back to the water at Harold lying out another net. Within the hour that was on the hillside each lady finished filling two six gallon buckets full of berries.

"Eemmillyy!" Harold calls out. I run down the slope towards him but I get stopped by some really muddy patches that direct me farther inland and then back to the bank where he is.

"You need to eat." Harold says cutting a whitefish open over a tin bowl. Silvery, glossy eggs spill out of the fish onto the tundra. Spikes of grass in a circle frame the eggs.

"Try this," he says the twinkle in nis eye glimmering like the glossy eggs. I shovel the sweet, salty eggs into my mouth.

"Wait, you need to wash your hands," he says putting out a basin of fresh rainwater and a var of soap. Cleanliness is higher on their list of priorities than it is on mine. I wash quicky to resume eating the tasty eggs.

"You should wash your face too. Why is your hair…wet?" Harold asks slowly.

Leslie put some oil in my hair last night," which satisfies his inquisition. I wash my face and ty to eat again. This time he doesn't stop me. The eggs taste so sweet and salty I just about eat them all.

"Don't eat too much," he says furrowing his eyebrows together.

"Why?" I ask fearing they'll make me sick.

"Let me boil some of the meat," he says preparing his Coleman stove. "Aren't you tired?" he asks looking at me suspiciously. I was running around on the hillside but it felt great.

"No. Do you think I was wasting my energy?" I ask instantly regretting my question. A shadow falls over his face I hadn't seen before.

"Sometimes Patricia and I go camping alone. The boat is dirty. Why don't you sweep it out like a woman.?" Harold says coldly.

Quickly I walk to the boat blushing. Looking in the boat I realize there is no broom.

"With what?" I ask looking back at Harold fussing over his fish an d the ladies still bend over picking blackberries on the hillside.

"Use the grass," he says impatiently. So I rip a bunch up and fold it into what turns out to be a good broom. Proudly I sweep the boat from a very dirty bottom to one that you could eat off. Harold inspects from his tiptoes along the shore. Now I get to eat some of the hot fish.

"Do you think the fish are in the net?" Harold asks coolly.

"Yes?" I say having no idea. He must agree because we get back into the boat to check the net.

"Are you strong?" he asks as we near the net. I pause wondering if this is a trick question. I know they think I'm a skinny wImp but I can do ten pull-ups on a good day. "Sometimes." I say.

"You're strong? I am strong," he says proudly as he starts to pull up the net. The water drips off in big chunks from the empty net. I feel my face starting to blush again feeling this might be an awkward situation. Harold's square body pulls harder bringing up more net. To my relief the fish start to drip off the net like the water was. I stare frozen in the boat. The net is covered by layers of fish.

"Pull them off!" Harold orders. Clumsily I untangle the fish from the net as Harold keeps pulling up more netting which moves us across the channel. I can't keep up with him. The fish are flipping at our feet sliming up my nice sweeping job. I try to step closer to Harold for a better angle but I slip instead making him laugh.

"Oh look what's coming!" he sounds like a kid on Christmas morning. A flat, round fish comes up. He grabs it in his hand and flings it. It spins like a Frisbee until it belly flops forty feet from the boat.

"They like that. It's a lush fish," Harold advises me. We're half way through the net and the floor of the goat is covered with flapping fish ~ two fish high all flipping and flopping.

"Oh no! It's a biting fish. Grab the bat! His it on the head!" I stare at the two feet long fish biting at the net with what looks like three rows of teeth including teeth on his tongue. I start swinging but I don't have the killer instinct.

"Harder! You have to hit it on top of the head!" Harold says laughing at me feeble swings. I hit it hard ending its struggle. Harold freezes in surprise. I smile also surprised.

We pull up more as my proficiency increases. At first some of the fish were getting away at the last minute flipping on the edge of the boat back into the water. With one hand on top of the fish and the other on the bottom my nails dig a little into the side so they won't slip forward of back ward. Another lush fish comes up. Harold takes the honors of throwing ut again like a Frisbee. He seems so delighted with it I wonder if the fish does like it. Their flying saucer shape suites their momentary flight through the cloudy day back into the sea.

Just as we're finishing up my back starts to ache from my bent position for twenty minutes.

"Are you tired?" he asks hopefully. Thankfully I can answer yes.

"Let's go check on the ladies," he says glowing. We look at all the fish still flopping at our feet. The only place to sit is next to the motor.

We head the 1/8 of a mile over to the shore but they're still picking so we set to work on the canvas tent that will keep us dry over the boat tonight. I glance over at the women looking so peaceful and intent on their work. All three of them huddle close to the Earth but spread out in tier own space on the soft orange colors of the tundra. It's a chameleon landscape changing by the different lighting of the skies moods.

Harold and I setting up the tent is another story. I resign helping unless he gives me specific instructions because he keeps retying any knot I learned as a boat captain or from rock climbing with excessively over tied knots. Somehow he makes an A frame tent out of the three long sticks and tarp. Some of the fish are still flapping their tails. Harold has placed most of the fish in bags and left the fish for dinner out on the grass. I marvel at the whitefish still moving its gills desperately trying to breath. I lean closer. Th grass tip pricks my cool cheek.

"I think I feel a little like you do," I whisper to the silver, glimmering fish, grasping for air out of water.

The ladies descend the hillside just before dusk with more berries than I have seen in one grouping even at a farmer's market. It only took a few hours.

After a nice meal of boiled whitefish I hike out alone towards the top of the hill. It takes ten minutes to reach it and see what's left of the remaining landscape in the low light. A dark blue/gray is falling over the tundra turning the rusty colors to black. Everything looks so smooth, even and still across the endless tundra.

There's a comfortable and relatively dry spot on top of the hill. I sit down out of view of my companions and pick a few black berries for dessert. They are semi-sweet. My teeth relax in mid chew resting the waxy skin of the berry on my tongue allowing the juice to spill out. I think Daniel would say that blackberries special power is to make you miss your loved ones. The blackness on the land spreads up across the air and all around felling heavy. I keep looking trying to see anything out on the expansive tundra but it just gets darker and darker.

I hear a light wind from my still position and look up to see an owl swooping overhead. It circles quickly and then dives towards me. My fingers press into the cool, moist ground getting me to my feet as the owl circles again and then dives. Crouching and running back down the hill as the owl continues to chase and dive at me. Faintly, I hear the ladies calling my name. They get louder as I get closer but I still can't see them. My shoes sink into the land a little letting me know the water is close. The swooping owl leaves me as my companions come into sight.

"We were getting worried about you."

"You must have been near that owl's nest." Cheryl, the older and more candid woman days. At first that seems like a strange notion for an owl to have her nest on the ground but then again there are no trees or even bushes for a long, long, way.

The night doesn't get any better when I'm sent to sleep in the bow of the boat where the tarp doesn't reach. Cheryl volunteers to sleep down from me but I'm the only one exposed to the sky which will probably rain and I'll have to step over five people if I need to get out to pee. We all get situated under our blankets in the boat like sardines.

"I hope I don't think you're my husband," Cheryl says half seriously, half lightheartedly. I smile rolling over to try and adjust my bones on the planks of the metal boat. Sleep does not come easily but sure as the Sun rises in the east, my bladder begins to press on me half way through the night. Unless I want to wake five people up or go for a swim, I'm stuck.

Thankfully the Sun does rise after what feels like three nights.

"You were pushing into me last night," Cheryl says in a way that I can't tell if it really bothered her or she thought it was funny. Either way I apologize but am solaced that I must have slept if I don't remember that.

Today is more of what we did yesterday except that it seems like we have all the fish we can fit in the boat and the ladies are done with the berries. Harold continues to asak me if I'm tired and tells e I should take a nap. I'm not tired. I want to get home so I can call my mom and tell her I'm alive, I mean…safe and sound.

"The weather isn't good. We need to wait." Harold keeps saying.

"But there is school tomorrow," I plead looking at the sky which looks like the same overcast sky we traveled in yesterday.

"Being safe is more important than school," Harold states. Even the other three women start to ask Patricia to get us going after we eat lunch. Patricia just re-braids her long hair right to the tip sitting on the cushion of all the plastic bags then knots it up to curl it and secure the braid on top of her head.

Paranoia starts creeping over my mind like someone shot the back left side of my brain with Novocain. I like down on the plastic bags next to Patricia pretending to be tired and take a nap. Satisfied with my five minute napping performance, Harold decides it's time to go home.

At first everything goes smoothly except that it's really cold and the rain starts to come down pretty hard in the uncovered boat so Patricia takes the job of wiping Harold's lenses whenever he takes them off his face which is every few minutes.

"Aren't you cold? Gusuks always get so cold," the ladies keep saying. I look at them all huddled up with their backs to the rain thinking they don't look too warm. I can feel my lips turning blue but I assure them I am fine. I'm always fine. Although I'm so cold it's hard to move my mouth to tell them that I'm fine.

Sitting in the stern of the boat facing the back towards our camp site I begin to focus on Daniel. I focus my breathing concentrating on the beat of his heart. I focus on images with eyes closed when he's with me. Bright colors on delicate flowers. Butterflies gently, slowly and deliberately flapping their wings. Bright green pastures of clovers waving in a sunny breeze. Dolphins jumping, flying, suspending in the air. Magnified blades of grass juicy and plump. A view from a mountain top watching a huge waterfall streaming down against the rock in slow motion. The spray rises up and out with the wind. Eagles rising over a cliff edge so close that their velvety feathers almost tickle me. Just quick glimpses like a theater turning on suddenly and then back to black. With another kiss another bright flash of colors. This picture is an ocean so calm and blue in the bright, white Sun. I'm not afraid of what's below. A flash of a whale's ancient eye. What would it be for Daniel to be here? To stay warmly with him. He moves closer like the waves rolling on the ocean.

"Emily. Are you all right?" Harold asks faintly. I stay focused.

"Emily, are you cold?" Harold asks a few minutes later. I stay staring at the waves. Daniel stays keeping me warm.

"Emily, what are you doing?" Harold asks getting nervous and becoming a nuisance. I glance at him quickly to let him know I'm well and then resume my focus.

Wump! The boat jerks back as the engine grinds up some sand. My whole body shivers. Good-bye Daniel.

We're still probably a few hours from Edinak with land a few miles to the east of us and what looks like the whole open sea west of us. The women move to the bow to take the weight off the engine so we can back up a little but id doesn't work. Patricia takes a stick and pushes us backwards which frees us from the sand we're on to get us stuck on another section. The waves lap against the small boat. I feel a shipwreck coming on. We won't go hungry with all this fish but I don't know how much water they brought. I only have two liters.

Carla grabs the other stick and helps push as Harold tries the radio. Broken. My breathing quickens but I keep my mouth closed. Harold starts up the engine again and we break free making it smoothly farther towards the land only to get stuck again. The same routine works this time but the next time the water looks only two feet deep but very clear showing a smooth, fine grain sand below.

"We have to lose some weight," Patricia says finally speaking up. All eyebrows rise. My throat clenches fearing it will be me. Harold grumbles a bit but complies by throwing some of the fish back which helps but not enough. My mind starts to race wondering about the path we taking back. If we'll make it back and that there isn't a radio to call for help even if there was someone to help.

Harold throws out another bag of fish as we all push against the sticks to make some progress but we don't. My fingers grow cold from the water splashing while pushing with the stick. I've had this feeling before that it's all over but this time it feels more real and like it's going to happen slowly. I move my eyes across the stark horizon filled in with lots of cold water keeping tears from welling up. I retrace my scan back to something sticking out of the water. Something else pops up near to it. Leaning out a little more I can see seals. Hope. I continue to push and watch the seals and find myself smiling when I see another and another emerge. Their sleek heads and necks hold strong above the water. They start coming up closer an closer so that I can see the seals big, black, sweet eyes saying it's all right. Don't worry. Everything will be okay. My nerves calm down a level from extreme anxiety to a fear where logic still exists. We have food and some water. The weather could clear enough for Carla's husband to come looking for us in his plane like he did on our trip out yesterday.

The seals continue to come up and dive down curiously watching the boat with a pile of black plastic bags and six people floundering inside pushing off the sand. Carla, Sheryl and Hazel seem worried but Harold and Patricia just seem irritated. By the fourth time we get stuck we're all pretty good at getting unstuck. Harold pilots us out towards the seals and then back down a deeper canal but not by much. I start taking the navigating into my own hands watching the water's depth and the Sun's direction. I want to see if we stay in a consistent path no that I know what it should be but my participation makes me feel a little better as the Sun gets closer to the western horizon. Slowly the seals drift out of sight behind us. Silently I thank them for their presence. Maybe they were eating the fish we lost.

Just after dusk we make it back to the narrow canals of Edinak. The lights in the houses look very welcoming to my shivering body despite the three coats the women wrap around me from the bags. Plus they huddled around me tightly. I help Harold and Patricia by the light of their house with the bags until Will comes out. He looks big, strong and huggable moving gracefully and quietly from the boat to the house making my struggles with the fish look like a piece of cake. He looks at me with a hint of appreciation but also questioning so I stop bringing the fish in which is fine by me.

"Do you want to steam?" Patricia asks me. Harold supports her. "Emily, you should steam. Your hair is…wet."

"No thank you. I better get back and call my mom."

"You can stay here," Patricia offers.

"I better get back. Thank you though." I also thank God we're back.

I remember the four hour time difference and it's eight o'clock so instead of calling home I jump in behind Sophie to steam next to my house. The heat feels almost as good as my focus did on Daniel. It takes three times to wash my hair before I get all the dirt and baby oil out. The clear rinse water in my basin is proof.

I sleep hard too tired to dread Monday morning.

Chapter

"You win me!" Ingrid says to me after I tell her I went to Nelson Island. "I've been here all my life and never gone there and you've been here two weeks and went," she says with mock anger. Patricia walks by with some breakfast in the supply lounge area where I'm making copies.

"No, we didn't go that far," Patricia says but I don't get an answer as to where we did go. I finish the copies for research guidelines and head down the hall with Ingrid. Her vacation last week has her ready to take on the class.

Surprisingly the class takes the research guidelines with curiosity, possibly because Ingrid hands them out. Most of them select a book or two that they need from the rack of resources I wheeled in for them. All until Arie figures out someone turned the water on in the room for the sink and water fountain.

"The water is on!" Aaron, Joseph and Mark drop their books and race over to the running water. They turn it on high and then press their thumb inside the spout to spray water in all directions. I try to rescue any books and the comment/suggestion box I put over there when the water was not running.

Ingrid over powers my efforts to calm them down with some Yup'ik orders that are much more effective. Aaron comes back with his dad who turns the water off. I wonder who turned the water on.

"I'll get and elder to come in and talk to them." Ingrid tells me. The rest of the day is spent with Ingrid overpowering anything I say especially if the students show any sign of listening to me. If I made progress with the last week it's being …corrected now.

Defeated but at least not hungry from my mom's food Ihead over the boardwalk to the post office hoping to find a little salvation in a letter. Slowly turning the key to peak in the door I find two letters. I look around me like I found gold or in this case salmon in my PO box. Quickly I hide the letters in the inside packet of my coat and head home.

"Where are you going?" Mark asks me sitting with Ruvim part way back.

"Home." So they get up and follow me. My letters with have to wait. Stalin must have seen us from somewhere because by the time we get to my house they're all ready to come in.

"You don't have a sink," Mark says in his husky, strong voice. I look over to the sink in the kitchen.

"A place to wash our hands," he continues. So he takes my steam basin and fills it with water putting a bar of soap next to it with a towel and proceeds to wash his hands. Ruvim and Stalin look around at the barren surroundings with a little more reserve. After washing their hands they decide to sit down in the darkly lit corner where the kitchen table is. A propane lamp sits in the center. Quietly they start twisting the knob and looking around the base and inside the glass at the wick.

"I see my opportunity to teach without a protest. It's strange what the walls of a school do to the interaction between Yup'iks and Gusuks. I wonder if the Yup'iks would have built the building as it is.

"Do you want to light it?" I ask getting out a match. These are the same boys that flipped out over water today at school. Now they sit calmly as I show them how to light the lamp. A soft glow falls on the previously dark corner and the boys gaze at the dancing flame inside the glass making their black eyes glimmer like the color of dark rocks passing in and out of water. The blue at the base of the wick rises momentarily to a yellow tip the shape of a cat's tongue paintbrush.

Gently Stalin waves his hand over the top of the glass. He dares the flame to burn him, as his hand gets closer to the opening of the glass tube shrinking the flame and filling the glass with smoke.

"It's gonna go out," Mark warns alarming his two larger friends.

Ruvim just watches calmly. Stalin, the loud mouthed poet who's mother from the health clinic had said,

"It will never change. Never change." Maybe referring to Stalin getting people mad at him. He continues to test the flame putting his hand over the top of the glass blocking out all the air. The flame shrinks to a blue flicker.

"Don't!" Mark orders. Stalin laughs his deep laugh pulling his hand off shaking it around to cool. I let them continue their experimenting a few more times until Stalin tempts too far and the flame goes out. Mark sounds like his class self, "Cheeap."

"Why do you think it went out?" I ask lighting it again. They all look at each other and then at the flame. Stalin puts the flame out again.

"What do you take form the flame when you put your hand over the top of the glass?" We all watch entranced by the smoke curling, spinning and folding up out of the glass spreading out in the air and the dark corner.

"If you were in a plastic bag, what couldn't you do?"

"Breath!" Stalin exclaims.

"Right!" So what about the flame?" I ask lighting it again.

"It can't breath when Stalin keeps putting his hand over it," Mark says irritably.

"Yeah. Fire needs air to breath and burn. The three of them look at the flame. Stalin leaves his hand off the top while the other two flirt with the heat waving their hand over the top but neither of them suffocate it. Ring…ring.

"…Hello?"

"You're home!" my mom says delightedly.

"Yep. I'm here with some of my students." Mark and Stalin come over to see who it is.

"It's my mom. Do you want to say hi?" They nod their heads.

"Hello…good…Mark…eleven," he says handing the phone to Stalin who speaks an octave even lower than Mark but with the same curt conversation.

"Mom?" I ask.

"Their voices are so deep."

"I know."

"No, I mean rally deep."

"I *know*."

"That was almost eerie. My voice lessons in college said the stress and tension of our lives closes off our full vocal chords. That keeps us from our full voice, probably from what the Yup'iks sound like." She says.

"Yeah with a two hour steam every night, there isn't a lot of stress here."

"It's like they're speaking in a part of their souls from lives past," she says almost sounding scared.

"I suppose," I say not fully comprehending but I think I know what she means because I've never heard voiced as deep as theirs.

"You know I was reading more about the Eskimos or Inuits. They have lived farther north than any other people for thousands of years." She says.

"They don't call themselves Inuits ~ only Eskimos or Yup'iks. I look over to the three boys nodding.

"Well, it says Eskimo means eaters of raw meat," she says making me want a half cooked hamburger. "Let me go get the encyclopedia."

"Do you want us to take out your honey bucket?" Mark asks politely. I weigh the idea an say sure but feel a little uncomfortable.

"Okay, here it is…They lived by the sea and ate seals, whales and fish, sometimes caribou for meat and clothing and they made boats out of the skins. They got around by dog sleds and make houses out of sod or snow."

"Yeah I saw some of their mud houses from their ancestors but they laugh at the idea of living in igloos. Maybe that's just Ekinak or today though. We're not that far north for Alaska.

"Then their traditional way of life ended with the rifle and white trappers and white diseases," she reads.

"They still maintain some of their traditions. It would probably help if people like me weren't here making money off disturbing them. Although they have taught me a lot about being a Yup'ik. I think I would have to convert if I'm not to be a disturbance here. Mom…do you think it's right that I'm here?"

"I can't answer that for you but I think it's always good to finish what you start.

"What if what you start is wrong? Besides I haven't signed anything… I'm not even certified in Alaska yet."

"But they expect you to stay."

"The white people that hired me do but I really don't think the Yup'iks want white teachers unless they are married to a Yup'ik. I haven't deposited my check yet."

"Well I sent you another package of food so you can be on the look out for that."

"Okay. Thank you. Ken ken ken."

"What?"

"I love you." I say missing her very much.

"I love you too. Take care little sweetie." That's what my nonny calls me too.

The three boys wait outside talking with Cory and Anastasia. I wipe my eyes with the towel Mark just put out for the sink and head out with some Hershey's Hugs that I bought in Bethel. Anastasia likes them. She takes one smiling warmly. When people smile here, the smile grows slowly and lasts for a few precious moments, then if fades back into the heart that it grew from leaving a shining light in their eyes. The smiles here are soothing.

The boys don't want any chocolate but I ask Cory to get me some water. It's the first time I've seen him smile up at me. He fills my bucket from the barrel outside that's full of rainwater. It's important for people to have work to feel good. I know. I miss feeling helpful and useful.

We all part. I head back in to read my letters. First I open Kellie's letter wondering what in the world am I doing in Alaska. Her letter makes me laugh calling me a free spirited freak and telling me about her never ending boy troubles.

My letter opener tucks under the corner of Daniel's envelope and rips the edge open neatly. I sink into the couch.

Two more weeks and he will be off to South America for five months. That seems so long. In my journal I write: I want everything to be good. Is Daniel sweet talking me? I'll see. I'm not quite like the Yup'iks. I miss my friends. I like our craziness as the fifth graders put it. Tonight at the steam I felt like Dorothy in the Wizard of Oz trying to open the cellar door having it bang shut with the power of the wind. Except tonight it was the steam door to the cooling room. The wind is shaking the house. Anuuqa = wind.

Despite my mom's food my skirt still felt looser today. Tuesday. The day Dick, the psychologist is coming to Edinak.

"Don't send Aaron with him," Ingrid tells me, her eyes looking very serious thought her big glasses. Great the student that's given me so much resistance is the sone of my aid and the one I'm least worried about getting bothered by this man.

"You can take Helen, Stalin and Joseph." I tell Dick outside in the hall while Ingrid gets the rest started on the research project for their states of choice. Dick towers over me stroking his brown mustache. "Oh I just take boys." He says.

"Well Helen has had the most problems with me and the other kids, making fun of Nina for wearing a dress. Crying hysterically when I tried to talk to her about hurting Nina's feelings and a lot of other similar instances. Why won't you take her?"

"I think it's better to keep counseling sessions within a same sex boundry." He says. These are fifth graders and Helen is usually at recess with the boys anyway.

"I've been working with Ruvim the last few years and would like to continue with him." He says. I can hear Ingrid trying to help the kids peacefully behind me.

"Okay." I say regretfully.

Not only do I mess up the research project's progress with my presence but Ruvim who had started to accept me as at least a person if not his teacher scowls at me as he walks out with Dick, Stalin and Joseph. A soon as I enter the scene Aaron leads the class in the disposal of their research projects.

I speed walk to the post office at the end of the day. Another letter from Daniel is just as moving as the others. I feel like when I give blood from not being near him. Like I need to eat a lot of juice and Oreos to regain my strength. Instead I head over to the Ardok's. The serenity prayer seems to be staring out daring me...

'God grant me the serenity to accept the things I cannot change.

Courage to change the things I can and the wisdom to know the difference.'

The injured puppy is back on four legs with a limp but he's feeling up to licking my hand.

Harold and Patricia greet me inside with a beautiful coat made of caribou, mink, beaded designs and leather strips of fur collar, interior and wrists. It reaches down below my knee.

"You need a man and you can get a coat like this. You're coat won't keep you warm this winter," Harold tells me. I'm sure they have just the man for me but my heart already belongs to Daniel. I don't stay long.

"Hi Mom. They're ready to marry me here."

"What is your purpose there?"

"To teach."

"Is that what you're doing?" she asks softly.

"No."

Wednesday morning arrives after a restless night of sleep. I just want to be held by Daniel. IT's like the whole world is a tornado but when he's holding me safe.

The morning is bearable because Ingrid finds an elder to talk to the kids and she does. The elder woman sits down in front of the room and the kids sit up as if a metal pole runs down their spines. She talks to them soothingly in Yup'ik for an hour and a half and none of them protest of hardly blink. She talks them right into recess. I have no idea what she says but I like the sound of it.

The afternoon is a little productive because Ingrid found some reading volunteers but the kids don't want to read the books about Gusuk children.

I go into T.J.'s office at the end of the day.

"Hello, how's your day going?" he asks pleasantly even though he looks like he's up to his elbows in alligators again.

"Fine but I don't think I'm a good teacher here." He leans back in the chair like an alligator is approaching him.

"I haven't gotten any complaints about you which is more than I can say for some other teachers." He says.

"They like me but they don't respect me," I say choking on my words a little, trying not to cry. T.J. Flinches.

"Well, we can get some more help in there."

"No, they just don't want me to teach them. It's not appropriate for me to teach them," I say starting to cry.

"Oh, it's okay. I don't even know all the student's names yet and in all my years I've been teaching that's the first thing I do," he says handing me a tissue.

"Me too," I blurt out between sobs.

"Okay, okay, it's all right. You'll be okay," he says calming me down a little.

"Well how much time do you want to give this?"

"I'll stay until Friday but I've already figured out they don't want me to teach them," I say trying to calm down.

"So you've decided."

"Yes. And when the psychologist comes back I don't want him to work with Ruvim anymore.

"Okay, I'll see to that."

"Thank you." I say feeling my take flight instinct growing strength. I punch my time card. They said they'd pay me $13 an hour to sub. That should pay for my ticket and rent while I've been here.

I call Daniel before the steam to tell him I'm coming back.

"Don't do that. I'll come up there."

"No it's not good for me to teach here. They want their own people to teach. I don't want to tell the Ardoks I'm leaving though.

"They'll probably be surprised if you stay. Did you get a flight back?"

"Yes, I had bought an open ended ticket luckily and Jen is finished with work in Denali so she can pick me up for my lay over in Anchorage Saturday afternoon." Jen is a friend from Glacier from the previous winter when I taught winter ecology.

"I'll pick you up," Daniel says sounding like he's containing his excitement…I hope.

Miraculously Rich, the special education teacher, shows up to consult with me for the first time since I've arrived. His wife, Belinda wants to take the class and she's Yup'ik and only a few courses away from certification and can fulfill her practicum while teaching the class. I am so happy to hear that.

Ingrid has a little different reaction when I tell her I'm leaving.

"You can't leave me!" she exclaims pointing to the lesson plan book and grades. "Look they have grades. They are reading!"

"You're the one that knows what they need. You should be the teacher." I say lovingly.

"But I'm not certified." We both pause looking each other straight in the eyes and smile to the point of laughing over our honest assessment with no grudges.

The intercom system buzzes me to T.J.'s office so Ingrid continues teaching the math lesson that is now going very well with her in front of the room.

"The people in Bethel want to talk to you," he says handing over the phone.

"Hello?" I ask nervously.

"Hello, Miss Strauss. We've been informed of your decision to leave and we would like you to reconsider. If you break a contract we will dock you two weeks pay and revoke your Alaska teaching certificate. Teaching is a hard profession and if you can't make it here there is no reason you will anywhere else."

"I don't have an Alaska certificate. I haven't signed a contract. You hired me as a substitute so I expect to be paid as a substitute. I don't know if you've been here but Edinak doesn't want Gusuk teachers and I am not going to disturb and use these people to make $34,000. I've taught in a lot of different situations very successfully and it's wrong for me to stay here." I finish glancing at T.J. who has a slight smirk on his face. He must not like this fellow either. I wait for the silence to end.

"Well, I'm going to recommend that you don't get an Alaskan teaching certificate."

"Goodbye."

The hard part after school is telling the Ardoks. When I told the students they wanted to know who their new teacher would be and were delighted when I told them Belinda would be their teacher. Trenton, her nephew, especially.

I enter the Ardok's house. They walk out of their bedroom looking a little groggy.

"I'm sorry. Did I wake you?"

"No, no come in and have some akutaq," Harold says. So we all sit at the table in their bright kitchen with a drying rack full of dishes. Patricia passes out three bowls of akutaq. I feel relief knowing I won't have to have this as a major part of my diet for too much longer.

"We wondered what you were doing. I thought maybe our trip was too much for you," Patricia says. It was a big adventure.

"No, I've just been busy. I've decided to go back to Montana." They both pause and look at each other reflectively.

"You're not staying?" Harold asks.

"No," I say touched by the sadness that has fallen over their kitchen.

"What do your parents say?" Patricia asks.

"They're supportive." Harold looks to Patricia.

"They're being protective?" she asks.

"Yes." I look at them – first Patricia then Harold.

"Do you want your people to teach your children?"

"Yes," Patricia says definitively. I haven't heard so much resolution here as from her response to that question.

"Would you like me to write about that?"

"Yes," she says again with certainty.

Leslie goes home with me to help me clean and pack. She looks in my jewelry box and places a silver and turquoise ring inside the wooden box. I take out a silver and onyx ring and give it to her. She points to the pearl ring my Nonny once wore smiling.

"No, my grandma would be upset if I gave away her ring that she gave to my mom who gave it to me," I say also knowing I don't want to give it up. Although I will miss Leslie.

"Will you write?"

"Yes. Put your address in that book with the cat on it."

"I'll put my birthday too," she says smiling her Cheshire cat smile.

The next morning, I start to work training Belinda in what I've done showing her the lesson plans, grades and writing samples. Her speaking voice is as nice as her singing voice that I'd heard in church. Her husband comes in still trying to get me to stay while the scoots him away. I leave them to their discussion and approach Anastasia leaning over the copier looking sadly out the window at the gloomy day. She turns to me with glassy eyes.

"I wish my son could have come home like you are doing." She says almost crying but she remains stoic. She looks back to the tundra leaning her body on the copier. I want to hug her but quietly walk away.

I don't want to show tears either. Following her lead…mirroring, honoring her strength and stoicism.

Lee is surprisingly not at his desk and instead having a cup of coffee in the supply/lounge room.

"How do people live to be so old in the Bible?" he asks out of the blue.

"Maybe they didn't know how to count," I say making him chuckle.

"Actually I think they had a different calendar than we do now so it sounds like they lived a long time but I think they lived shorter lives than we did but I'm not sure," I say surprised again by a question.

Belinda makes it through the day giving the kids hugs here and there. Trenton is smiling instead of scowling. I tell Ruvim and Belinda that he won't have to go with Dick anymore. My guess was right that Ruvim didn't like going there because he gives me a nod of approval. At least I corrected that mistake.

After school I invite Donna over to take the leftover food I have. I help her out the arctic door with the food and mud boots that are too big for me when Sophie greets us.

"There's a seal party! You haven't been to a seal party. You have to see it before you go," she says waving her arm emphatically to follow her. Donna heads home but I race after Sophie on the boardwalk to the northeast side of the village where it looks like all the females in the village where it looks like all the females in the village are standing seemingly waiting for something.

Sure enough through this afternoon's almost sunny sky flies a bunch of little candy pieces sailing in an arc overhead. I look up as all the women stand throwing out buckets of candy to the crowd. It's the Joner's seal party — a girl in the fifth grade. Gleefully I pick up all the pieces around my feet like the women around me.

Next they throw out hand towels followed by plastic bags — each toss creating a sea of hands reaching up to the sky. They throw out enough stuff to fill a domestic section of Wall-Mart. Each throw sends up shouts of joy. I hear one woman say to a new mother with a baby girl,

"I wished I'd had a baby girl."

The two women coo over her until the next set of close pins flies into the air. They rise against the cirrus clouds starting to paint a beautiful sunset over Edinak. The red, orange and pink in the sky make the greens on the tundra brighter and the blue on the houses softer. A humid and refreshing breeze helps us stay cool as we clamor for gifts falling from the sky.

Tonight can't pass too quickly. I trace back through the episodes of the days spent here ending with the girls and I sitting on the arched bridge. It's the first starry night I've seen here. The stars look closer and brighter than I can ever remember seeing them. Almost like they're in 3D.

"You could just stay and Daniel could come here," says one of the seventh grade girls.

"What would we do?" We all pause peacefully wondering at the twinkling stars surrounded by black.

"Just be together."

"Maybe we can come back and visit."

"That would be good."

At least I'm with Daniel in my thoughts. I struggle to fall asleep and have the time pass more quickly.

I must have fallen asleep because the Sun greets me shining in through the honey bucket room even before my alarm goes off. I make haste getting my stuff together and out the door. I stand there blankly wondering how to get my bags the half a mile to the runway. I suppose I could carry them individually but that seems like a lot of work and I'm worried about missing the plane.

It's the stillest I've seen the village and the sunniest. I almost understand how the students felt on the other partially sunny day cursing the Sun's brightness. I snap out of it and tilt my head up closing my eyes to soak it in. A noise from two houses over opens my eyes. It's Carl's dad who looks as equally groomed as Carl does.

"Could you take me to the runway?" I ask pleadingly pointing to my bags.

"The Bethel plane won't be here for an hour. You should have taken Wayne's flight this morning form here," he says which I hope he's wrong about because then I'll miss my plane to Anchorage.

"That's okay. I'll just wait there," I say feeling a little more anxious. Begrudgingly he starts his ATV up and loads up my three big bags. I sit on the back as we drive down the boardwalk on the prettiest morning since my arrival. He drops me off without a word. Strangely my normally thin skin lets this roll off my back. I'm just grateful he took me to the runway.

The first ten minutes I wait impatiently looking at the sky to the east where Bethel sits. No sign of any plane, only a flock of ducks flying over in a neatly aligned V. I look at my watch calculating how much time I can afford to lose. Only about another half hour. Then I could get on the noon flight from Bethel and meet Jen in Anchorage. Ten more minutes pass. Nothing. No one is even out in the village.

Making myself comfortable I surrender to hope for the best. Don't fear Ruth would say. A surprising serene and soothing blanket falls on my heart. I slump on the soft, army bag looking at Edinak. The perfectly still village of plywood houses on stilts. It's illuminated by the morning Sun nestled in the tundra by the sea. The picture where my arrogant youth found some humility.

My time feels suddenly taken, vanquished like the life from the fish gasping in the grass. There's the plane. It soars in the blue. I catch my breath. Glancing back at Edinak, Harold's words echo of his real people. It's true but they're not the only ones.

The sound of the plane's engine takes me from my trance. I look at my watch. Only an hour before the next plane takes off from Bethel and there are people getting off this plane with luggage. That will take some time. I catch my breath. Glancing back at Edinak, Harold's words sing softly now. "We are the real people." He told me leaning in over the kitchen table challenging me…but lovingly. The generous salty, fragrant fish that they prepared warm and ready to eat between us.

Now I slump again on my luggage knowing how grateful I am to them and that I will miss them.

Finally the bush plane is deboarded. Hopping up to drag my duffel bag, I ask the young Gusuk pilot, "I have to get on a noon flight from Bethel. Do you think we'll make it?" I ask trying to hurry him.

"Oh yeah…I'll get you out of this camping trip." He says smiling. The plane takes off towards the sea and then circles back heading east. I get a last glimpse of the village surrounded by the loud sound of the engine on the plane. The village looks so still but the zaring engine takes the peace from the houses and winding board walks below.

On this sunny day I have a better view of the sky but we still fly low so the landscape looks like the same snaking water ways but today it's just more well lit. It looks pretty. Shiny even.

Crane my neck more to see if Bethel is coming into view but it's more tundra and a couple smaller villages. I know it won't be for at least another twenty minutes and it's 11:35 already.

Finally when I'm feeling trapped by the stale air of the plane Bethel comes into view as well as the airport. A bigger plane is taking off before us so we circle and then land.

That was my plane. My heart sinks. I don't know it for sure but I do.

With a metal plate feeling in my chest I get off the crouched plane and head inside to see if my connection was the plane that just took off. It was. The young pilot follows me in looking a little sorry.

"My airline has another plane going to Anchorage in a half hour. I could put your stuff on that plane and you can go to the desk and see if they'll transfer your ticket." He offers encouragingly. Sounds good to me. I walk over to his airline. My hopes drop a little when I see the Yup'ik women behind the counter looking at me sourly.

"Hello, I just got off your Bush flight from Kipnuk and it arrived late so I missed my connection to Anchorage. The pilot said I could get on your next flight." I say trying to sound confident while feeling totally desperate.

"No." All three women just stare at me harshly, rigid and closed-mouthed. It feels like the must of Bethel is choking me plus the glares of these ladies who want to do anything but help me.

I walk outside feeling the tension of a tin suit clutching my bones. I don't want to miss Jen although I could probably find another place to stay but the thought of seeing a friend is very comforting to me right now.

Back in the vestibule I was dropped off at, a very pretty, Yup'ik woman is calling for the last borders for flight 209. She looks so pleasant and friendly, proudly wearing her navy uniform. A few other people board as she asks them for their names, checking them off on a piece of paper. I sit feeling like a bomb ready to explode wondering if that's the plane going to Anchorage and if my stuff is on it. The young pilot is nowhere to be seen.

"Last call for flight 209." She says to the nearly empty room of vinyl seats. She looks so much friendlier than the other women. Proud of her hourglass figure in her fitted uniform, shoulder length hair, and showy make-up on. I get up and walk towards her without really breathing.

"Name please?" she asks pleasantly.

"Alison" I say rather tersely without stopping.

"Thank you." She looks down at her list. My stride increases towards the plane looking forward. I board without looking the stewardess in the eye and head to the back of the plane where there are a few empty seats. Just take off. Please nobody ask me for a ticket. Once we are in the air I try to figure out if we are headed east which I think we are but just to make sure I lean forward to the passenger ahead of me.

"Is this going to Anchorage?" I ask trying to sound blase. Don't think I fool the middle aged man into thinking that's an ordinary question but he doesn't admonish me.

"Yes." he answers simply. Okay, one out of three obstacles solved. Now if my luggage got on the plane and if Jen will wait for me.

Please Jen wait for me. I focus on Jen's face. Her multi-colored eyes, full lips and shiny, straw colored hair. So thick and long like a horse's mane. I think about how we'd stick our faces in the huge snow drifts to make molds for something to do on a Friday night in the isolation of our winter in West Glacier. I think how she taught me to make pizza with homemade dough and how I'd dance around making her laugh for our evening entertainment without a TV or phone. Please Jen wait for me. Mostly I focus on her quirky personality that said whatever she thought no matter how blunt and her artistic eye that could find beauty in a back alley of Chicago where she was a photography major.

The jagged white peaks come into view. Please Jen wait for me.

When they finally allow me off the plane the luggage has already been taken and I can't see if my stuff is there but I don't really care about it that much. I search the huge bright, sunshiny windows of the airport for Jen. Then pause walking in from the tarmac for a moment taking in the view of the majestic snow capped mountains all around me.

Now this is what I thought of when I pictured going to teach in Alaska. The hallway of this airport is big and practically empty. Like a happy walk down a bright hallway to The Wizard of Oz. The tile floor shines cleanly in the sunlight coming through the towering windows. I stand in front of the luggage conveyor belt for a sad moment but they are empty and not moving. All the people on the flight clear out with their rides or on their own. That familiar ache in my chest strengthens.

Waiting alone by the still luggage conveyor belts makes me scared so I walk farther down the hall where I find a standing wrack of luggage with my bags waiting on them! There's two out of three unknowns solved. Now where is Jen?

I continue down the long towering hall with my heavy bags dragging behind me. At the end I can go left or right. Two people are walking down the right hall at a distance which makes me think it could be Jen because of the woman's long hair and long, skinny legs. I speed up towards them trying to look casual in case it's not her.

"Emily?" I hear her sweet voice echoing down the mighty hallway.

"Jen!" I yell running down to hug her.

"Emmy!" she laughs hugging me tight.

"It's so good to see you!" I missed my plane so I thought I might miss you too!"

"Oh, no we were late too. Traffic. This is my friend Josh." Jen says of the sweet faced man standing next to her. I shake his hand enthusiastically, making him laugh too.

"Where do you want to go?" Jen asks.

"The grocery store!"

They help me with my bags out to their van and we head for a super duper market. I have never been so happy to be in a grocery store. Especially one that has lots of free samples. I sample everything at least once then buy some milk and chug it out in the parking lot.

Then I have Jen shower with me that night so we can wash each other's backs like the Yup'ik women did for me. Rocking me back and forth like a beloved baby curled up on the plywood boards.

Jen giggles at me with the idea but she obliges and I get to sweep her hair off her freckle free ivory back. Now I'm the mom and she's the baby.

We rise early in the morning so they can take me back to the airport so I can get back to Daniel.

"Are you sure you don't want to go to Denali with us for the week? Then we can all go back together?"

"Yes…I'd love to go but Daniel will be gone in a week for South America and I want to see him before he goes."

"Love makes ya stupid." Jen said smiling.

"Hey, I told you that." I chided back.

The flight takes off on time and I have a seat with a good view of The Rocky Mountains. I watch them like a trail taking me back to Glacier and to Daniel. It feels like I am meeting back up with my soul. Belinda had told me to listen to my heart. It was easy to do with the volume at which it was screaming at me to leave Edinak.

The Flathead Valley comes into view as I tell the nice business man next to me the good places to go while he's here because he doesn't hog the arm rest. I think my excitement is evident as I hold the Nalgene bottle with the blue lid of Edinak's Rain water I collected. Water drops of heaven funneled into waterfalls off the tin roofs. Saved and stored in metal barrels next to the arctic entrance side door.

"I'm sure your boyfriend is going to be happy to see you." The gentleman assures me on the plane.

"I hope so." I say looking at the airport willing us to get there faster.

We are a little early so I get my bags and search for Daniel outside on the welcoming cream colored sidewalk. Solid ground. Taking a deep breath… the air smells so good. I don't even remember exactly what he looks like but I recognize his 1987, white Jetta with the bumper tied on pulling up to the curb. He looks like Luke Skywalker in his white jet, the way his car fits tightly around him. His demure smile with his head tilted down is visible through the window even with his huge, dark sunglasses on.

Daniel gets out slowly pushing his sunglasses above his brow bone resting them there. I feel like a tree growing roots where I stand. He hugs me tenderly and the tornado stills. My roots melt away. He leads me to the passenger seat with his arm around my waist. Inside the car he hands me a bottle filled with hot springs water. Opening the blue lid smelling the sulfer springs. Taking a little sip. Gently, I hand him the bottle of rain water from Edinak. Matching blue lids. Softly, surprised by the same exchange. Both giving the gift of water.